All around you, screaming orcs leap from the wall, forcing the remaining pockets of resistance to retreat and reform around Fostyr at the opening to the underground tunnels.

You stagger toward your friend. Fostyr sees you and gestures wildly for you to hurry. As soon as you reach him, Fostyr claps you on the arm with his free hand.

"Get moving," he says. He grins wearily. "I was afraid they'd got you."

"What about you?" you say. "I can't just leave you!"

Fostyr takes a deep breath. "I'll hold them off while you and the others get away. Your mission is more important. Don't worry about me. Just go!"

You hesitate, not certain what to do.

If you retreat into the tunnels, go to 8.
If you stay and fight beside Fostyr, turn to 36.

Only your decisions can help you to survive the *Siege of the Tower!*

Endless Quest® BOOKS

Endless
Quest®
BOOKS

Siege of the Tower

Kem Antilles

A million thanks to Lillie E. Mitchell for her typing; Letha
L. Burchard and Paul Amala for their love of the
ADVANCED DUNGEONS & DRAGONS® game and for their
resourcefulness with spells and monsters; and my friends,
Kevin J. Anderson, Rebecca Moesta Anderson, Mark
Budz, Marina Fitch, and Michael Paul Meltzer, without
whom this book could never have been written.

—K.A.

SIEGE OF THE TOWER

First Printing: July 1994
Printed in the United States of America
Library of Congress Catalog Card Number: 94-60100

9 8 7 6 5 4 3 2 1

ISBN: 1-56076-894-0

TSR, Inc.
P.O. Box 756
Lake Geneva, WI 53147
United States of America

TSR Ltd.
120 Church End, Cherry Hinton
Cambridge CB1 3LB
United Kingdom

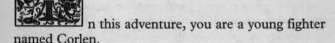n this adventure, you are a young fighter named Corlen.

You are seventeen years old, lean and well muscled from hard work as well as plenty of fighting practice. You stand just over six feet tall, with red, shoulder-length hair and stone-gray eyes set in finely chiseled features. Your friends say that you smile occasionally, but rarely laugh—with good reason.

Five years ago you had a curse placed upon you by the evil wizard Tyrion. As a result of this curse, you are unable to touch any kind of metal without suffering painful burns. Despite this handicap, you have become proficient in using a braided leather whip and flint-tipped arrows. For armor, you wear a leather breastplate. An oak practice sword hangs at your side; rarely used, the hard wooden blade is mainly for appearances, though you've given bullies a few painful whacks with it from time to time.

Here in your native Flanaess, you have been assigned to the border outpost called Dragon's Eye Tower. Constructed centuries ago of stone blocks, the isolated tower lies in the bleak frontier lands, between the vast Vesve Forest and the shore of calm Whyestil Lake, near the dreaded shadow of the evil land of Iuz. Few soldiers desire to be stationed in such a place, but you joined the army to protect the land, and you will go where you are needed most.

The outpost is quiet and mysterious, frequently

blanketed with ominous fog, and the sky is nearly always gray. The place is thick with shadowy history.

Dragon's Eye Tower got its name from a mysterious and powerful magical object, a petrified dragon's eye lost centuries ago in the winding, barely explored tunnels beneath the ancient structure. But now, after all these years, the Dragon's Eye has finally been found by another band of adventurers.

Rumors of the discovery have spread to dark Iuz, and the enemy is very interested indeed, because the eye holds great powers for those who know how to use it. Reinforcements have been summoned from the city of Crockport to the south, but it will take some time for an army to travel so deep into the wilderness.

In the meantime, you and the other soldiers at the tower must guard this precious talisman. Scouts have reported a great army of orcs approaching. The fortress is old and may not withstand such an assault, but you and the other fighters have vowed to hold it at all cost. The Dragon's Eye must never fall into the hands of the evil invaders. . . .

To save the Dragon's Eye, you must make the right decisions over the course of the story. The fate of the adventure lies in your hands.

Go right on to 2.

2

Facing into the cold wind, you lean against the high tower wall's worn, broken stone. You squint north toward the Dulsi River and the rocky shoreline of Whyestil Lake. You are tense and watchful. It has been this way for days.

Although nothing stirs in the forest below, you are uneasy as the shadow of Dragon's Eye Tower begins to melt into evening's cloudy gloom. Chill drafts seep through the chinks in the tower. The dreary weather has grown oppressive. You can't remember the last time you were warm and comfortable . . . certainly not since you came here to the tower.

If you had wanted comfort, you could have stayed in Crockport and found some kind of work that didn't require you to touch metal—as a street sweeper, perhaps, or a stable mucker. Instead, you chose to join the army and were assigned to the frontier.

Rumors of the approaching orc army fill you with dread and anticipation. Recently three scouts have returned to the tower with the same news; several other scouts haven't returned at all.

You finger your braided leather whip, shrug your bow higher on your shoulder, and continue to stare outward, ever watchful. "Just let them try to take the Dragon's Eye," you mutter under your breath.

Below, under heavy guard in the rusty cells of the stronghold, rests the newly found talisman. Though you cannot use the talisman's magic yourself, you have heard that the petrified Dragon's Eye allows a sorcerer to observe anyone or anything within a thousand miles. With such power, an evil sorcerer could direct his armies in surprise attacks, learn his enemies' every weakness. The artifact must be protected with your very life. That is your job.

You rub your eyes, then survey the earthen wall surrounding the tower, the newly built stables, and the Bloody Axe Inn. Other fighters on the east, west, and south watches shiver and pace at their posts. Everyone is silent, nervous. You look to the north again. Nothing has changed in hours.

A rock clatters behind you. You turn as Fostyr, your friend and comrade-in-arms, hurries to join you, cursing the rubble littering the tower. The tower is so ancient it is beginning to fall apart.

Fostyr huffs to a stop. He is young and whip-thin, with light brown hair and a frequent grin. "Any sign of them?" he asks.

"Not yet." You turn back to survey the shoreline.

Fostyr nods and peers into the murky distance. "A scout arrived from Vesve Forest about twenty minutes ago," he says. "He told Captain Jongh that the orcs are camped along the banks of the Dulsi. He says an orog named Gorak is in charge."

"Gorak?" you say. "I've heard of him. Isn't he the one who—?"

"Not him—*it!*" Fostyr's grin melts away into a thick voice. "Yes, Gorak's the one who tortured and killed my uncle." The hatred on Fostyr's usually cheerful face is doubly disturbing to you.

The two of you stand in silence, scanning the darkening horizon. Fostyr's words make you think of your father and his untimely death . . . and the curse that prevents you from touching metal of any kind.

Your father was the greatest sword maker in the city of Crockport, indeed in all the lands of the Flanaess. As his apprentice, you were well on your way to becoming a gifted sword maker in your own right. Your future seemed bright and secure.

Then the wizard Tyrion arrived, disguised as a mercenary, to commission a sword to be made for him. Your father, a hardworking and honest man, suspected nothing. In his smithy, he did his best work for the stranger—as he always did. He fashioned the blade with great care, then inlaid the blade with the strange characters Tyrion had meticulously drawn for him. Pretty designs, Tyrion had called them, a pattern his family had used for generations.

Unknown to you or your father, the characters were runes that would enable a wizard to wield the sword with great skill, even with little or no training in how to use it. Upon receiving the marvelous sword and admiring it in satisfaction in the sunlight that slanted through the open windows of the smithy, Tyrion whirled and struck down your father, christening the new blade with its maker's blood.

You remember rushing to your father, who lay facedown in the packed dirt, and crying out in disbelief.

You crouched there for a moment, stunned, before rage overcame your shock. In a blind fury, you snatched up another sword—one of the simple blades your father had you fashion for Count Delwyn—and you blindly attacked the wizard.

But Tyrion had merely laughed and worked a spell with his fingers, twisting a raven's-head ring on his left hand. Before you could reach the treacherous sorcerer, he placed an elemental curse on you. Suddenly the sword burned in your hands, too painful to hold. You stood staring at your red and blistering palms, the useless sword, and your dead father as Tyrion turned and casually walked away.

The thing you remember most clearly is Tyrion's smile of evil pleasure as he sheathed the rune-carved sword before strolling out the open smithy doors, leaving you to grieve over the body of your father. That smile has haunted you ever since. . . .

Now, standing atop the tower, Fostyr seems to

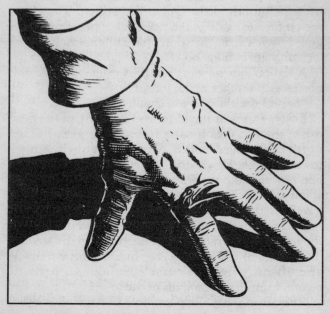

sense your brooding mood and says nothing, lost in his own unhappy memories. Together the two of you continue to watch the northern outskirts.

As twilight deepens, you see something glint in the distance where the Dulsi River runs into choppy Whyestil Lake. You frown. It could be a reflection of the fading daylight breaking though the clouds and sparkling on the water, or it could be an orc contingent fording the river. You concentrate on the river mouth.

"What did Captain Jongh say when he heard about the orc camp?" you ask Fostyr, your voice dry.

"That we no longer have the luxury of waiting for an armed guard to arrive from Crockport," Fostyr replies, a faint smile creeping over his face once more. "He's planning to send an escort out of the fortress with the Dragon's Eye in the morning. Somebody will have to take it to safety before the orcs get here."

You lean forward as two or three more glints flash near the mouth of the Dulsi. You stiffen. The glints are on the near side of the river and approaching. You grab Fostyr's arm. "We don't have till morning. Look! The orcs are coming now!"

A fighter on the west rampart cries out. "To the northwest! Torches in the forest!"

"Sound the alarm!" you shout.

Fostyr stares at the glimmers bobbing in the gray dusk, then dashes for the stairs. Your gaze flashes north to the river mouth, where more torches move toward you like slowly drifting embers. You shiver, certain now that the orc army will attack tonight. Unconsciously you check your weapons. This is what you have been waiting for, and dreading.

Within minutes, the alarm has sounded throughout the fortress. Down below, people bustle in the stables. The doors of the Bloody Axe Inn are thrown open, and off-duty fighters come rushing out. A shout echoes from the stone walls of the tower.

Remaining at your post, you narrow your eyes,

keeping the orc army in sight. Although you still can't make out individual orcs, the flicker of torches becomes brighter and more defined, dotting the flat-lands and the edges of the woods like fireflies.

Fighters swarm up the stairs to take their stations on the walls. Someone jostles you, and you grab the hilt of your oaken sword. Looking out over the earthen perimeter walls, you see the orcs pouring out of the north, giving up caution entirely.

Below, an explosion of curses and angry cries erupts in the courtyard. A weird, mocking laugh pierces the shouts, only to be cut off abruptly with a sharp gurgle of pain.

Fostyr elbows his way to your side. "What's going on?" you ask.

"An archer was caught trying to desert," Fostyr says. "He was a spy for Iuz."

You swear under your breath.

The orcs swarm closer. The flicker of the torches begins to merge into a single blaze.

Beside you, another fighter rushes up, panting with excitement. Her skin is flushed, and she blunders past, shrugging into a bulky shirt of chain mail. Instinctively you shrink from the metal mesh, but it grazes your arm and scorches your skin. You rub your stinging bicep, cursing, but your anger is directed toward the orcs, not the clumsy fighter.

Captain Jongh appears on the battlements and spots you, bustling forward as if he has a great many preparations to make and not nearly enough time. His nose is crooked from being broken and allowed to heal untended in a skirmish years ago. He claps you on the shoulder, narrowing his eyes.

"Corlen, Fostyr," he says, "we've got to get the Dragon's Eye out of here before it's too late. I need armed fighters I can trust to take the eye to Crock-port—in secret." He glares over the earthen walls at the approaching evil army; his twisted nose makes him appear almost as hideous as an orc. "But I also need people I can trust to stay here and defend the tower. I wouldn't lay odds on the success of either task, but somehow we have to accomplish both."

You look at Fostyr. You would like to stay with your friend, but you must make your own decision, for the good of the army. You grew up in Crockport and know the area well. But you are also one of the best archers in the guard and could inflict a great deal of damage when the orcs storm the tower.

"I won't order you to go with the Dragon's Eye," the captain says, "but if you do go, don't fool yourself. It'll be just as dangerous as staying here."

Fostyr looks to you for a decision.

Do you escort the Dragon's Eye, or do you stay and defend the tower?

If you decide to escort the Dragon's Eye to safety, turn to 25.

If you decide to stay and defend the tower, go to 23.

3

The scarred man claims to know the tunnels, but you don't really believe him. But you know even less about them, so you can't offer a better alternative.

You and the others follow the scarred man down the narrow left-hand branch. You bend to avoid bumping your head on the low ceiling as you enter the passage. Renda shuffles behind you, shoulders bowed by the weight of the wounded woman. Relf carries his sister's bow next to his own, slung across his back.

The scarred soldier scrambles confidently ahead. He twirls the end of the coiled rope at his side and waves his torch with the other hand. "Stay close to me," he says. "One wrong turn and you're lost. You could wander for days down here and never see the same passageway twice."

Already your neck and back ache from moving in such a stooped position. You wonder if you'll ever be able to stand up straight again.

Someone curses behind you. You turn to see Turloc, the flail wielder, rubbing the top of his head with one hand. The soldier behind him chuckles.

"Shut up!" In unrestrained anger, Turloc swipes at the second man with his torch. Sparks fly.

"He tried to set me on fire!" the second man complains.

"Enough!" you say sternly. "Stop it now, or neither one of you will make it out of here alive."

You make your way ahead. Ragged openings yawn in the tunnel wall at intervals, looking like toothed mouths. Gradually the tunnel narrows until your group must walk single file. The scarred fighter seems more and more uncertain about his path.

The stone walls press in on you, scraping your chest. The air is stifling. The musty smell of stagnant air coats your teeth and sticks to your tongue.

After a few more feet, the ceiling gradually lowers even farther, forcing you to crawl on your hands and knees. You hear the others gasp behind you. You break out in a cold sweat, and your head starts to spin. You can't seem to get enough air.

"I knew it!" the scarred man says somewhere ahead of you. "We made it! Come on." His voice bursts the bubble of nausea stuck in your throat.

A second later, cool, delicious air brushes your face and arms. The passageway widens abruptly, opening into a huge cavern. You stand, wincing at the pain in your stiffened back. Beside you, the others stand gasping, sucking in huge lungfuls of air.

You look around as your companions gather around the torchlight. The firelight flickers off daggerlike stalagmites growing up from the floor. Above each one, a matching stalactite descends from the ceiling. In places, the tips of the two meet, fusing together in hourglass-shaped sculptures.

"The Cavern of a Thousand Swords," Renda murmurs.

The blond man grins, his scarred eyelid adding a touch of menace. "It won't be long before we're out of here now," he says. "See? I told you so."

"Good job," someone says.

The rest chuckle, relieved and excited. A few people eat their last scraps of jerky as your party winds its way through the stone swords. After a few hundred feet, the cavern narrows, then widens again as several tunnels converge into a large chamber.

"This way," the scarred man says, leading you down the left-hand passage. He walks so quickly you have to jog to keep up with him.

Smaller stalactites hang from the ceiling like stilettos. You and your companions duck your heads as you thread your way through the rock swords. Every few feet another dark chamber hollows one side of the passages, leading to other tunnels. You walk for hours until you come to a **Y**.

The scarred man pokes his head into the left tunnel, which, you see over his shoulder, gradually slopes upward. He frowns. "That's odd. The right-hand branch is supposed to head upward, not the left-hand one. Ah, never mind . . . I see light ahead!" Confidently he starts up the left tunnel, motioning for you to follow him. "It's right—"

His torch jerks downward and his voice snaps off in a sharp gasp. The torch sputters as it strikes the sloped floor, rolling back toward you. You hear a muffled gasp rise and see a coil of black smoke as the torch struggles to keep burning.

"Help!" the scarred man rasps.

You lunge forward, Renda behind you.

The man hangs suspended by his fingers from the edge of a deep pit. The floor has ended abruptly in a sharp cliff. His eyes are wide in the light of the dropped torch, his face twisted as he struggles to hang on to the slick rock.

You grab for him just as his fingers slip free. You catch the loose end of the rope coiled over his shoulder. His weight jerks you to the ground, knocking the wind out of you and pulling you forward. The hidden Dragon's Eye digs at your chest.

Renda scrabbles forward on her knees, grabbing the rope. The scarred man's body slams against the side of the pit. He screams in panic.

"We've got you!" Renda calls down, pulling hard on the rope.

"Grab hold!" you shout, holding out your left hand toward him while continuing to hold on to the rope with your right.

The man reaches up. His hand is mere inches from yours when the rope suddenly uncoils from around his shoulder. He drops two feet before grabbing the rope again. The heavy lurch yanks Renda forward. She groans and digs her elbows into the ground, but they slip over the edge. Renda and the man's combined weight drags you toward the edge of the deep pit. You cling to the rope with both hands now, but the friction burns the skin of your palms.

"Renda!" Relf shouts, running forward.

Someone else grabs Renda's legs before she can slide over the precipice. She teeters on the edge. Relf squeezes in beside you and Renda, grabbing the rope.

"Hang on," you shout to the dangling man.

The scarred man's grip weakens. His mouth opens in horror as his hands begin to slip, slowly at first, then faster. He can't hold on. His feet kick against the side of the pit, searching for a foothold.

"Help!" he screams again, just as he plunges into the darkness. The rope goes limp. His cry ends with the sickening thud of his body far below in the pit.

With a shudder, you close your eyes and try to unclench your teeth. The muscles in your jaw hurt. Your right arm feels as if it has been ripped out of its socket. Sharp pain shoots through your shoulder as you push yourself back from the edge of the pit. You tried your best, but it just wasn't good enough.

You kneel, panting heavily. Relf helps Renda up. You blink at the light of the sputtering torch and glance back. Your companions crowd together at the tunnel entrance, anxiously peering inside.

Renda pulls up the rope. You grab the torch and stand up.

"Well," the soldier with the battle-axe says, "now what? Do we go on or turn back?"

You retrace your path to where the tunnels branch and peer down the other one, but you see only darkness. You could follow the second passageway, or you could make your way back to the Cavern of a Thousand Swords and the main tunnel.

If you decide to return to the Cavern of a Thousand Swords, go to 40.

If you choose to take the second branch, turn to 27.

4

You hurry deeper into the cave.

The sluggish air carries the stink of bat guano, dust, and mold. Ahead of you, patches of fungus grow on the walls, emitting a faint greenish-blue light. After a few feet, the ground evens out, becoming as smooth as stone. You test it with your heel. No wonder it feels so smooth. It *is* stone. You no longer hear any sound from the pursuing orcs.

You can move faster now on the even ground, and as your eyes adjust to the dim phosphorescence, you can even see where you are going. Suddenly one of your feet steps out over thin air, and you lose your balance as a black, unexpected chasm opens up in front of you. Your fingers frantically scrape the cave walls to keep you from falling. Awkwardly you sit down heavily with a grunt. Your boots touch something below you.

You find yourself sitting on a stairway—a steep one, carved out of the cave rock.

You push yourself to your feet and make your way down the stairs, grateful for the meager light cast by the strange fungus. At the bottom of the stairway, the tunnel angles to your left, then straightens. Another blast of foul air blows against your face.

Stifling as the air is, you're glad for the slight breeze. It means the cave doesn't come to a dead end. All you have to do is keep from getting lost.

The tunnel here is drier than you expected. You reach out, surprised to feel the rough texture of stone blocks. The faint glow of the wall fungus illuminates snakelike roots that have pushed through the joints between the stones. The roots remind you of gnarled fingers, holding the stones in place.

You pause to listen, but you still hear no sound of the orcs behind you. Maybe they've given up.

You take a breath between gritted teeth and push

ahead, your sword sweeping the darkness in front of you just in case something lies in wait.

The tunnel branches occasionally and also makes several sharp turns. Despite the turns, you seem to be heading south. If so, the forest should be on your right. You feel along the walls, finding more roots on the right side of the tunnel than the left.

As you walk, the loss of Fostyr weighs on you. You remember all the good times you had with the good-natured, whip-thin young man. It's as if part of you has died. His memory is still with you and will be for the rest of your life, but the future doesn't seem to hold the same excitement.

The clank of metal echoes down the tunnel from somewhere ahead of you. You tense. You grip your wooden sword more tightly, knowing you cannot go back the way you came. If you encounter an enemy up ahead, you'll have to fight here in the darkness.

You edge forward cautiously, uncertain how far ahead the noise came from. The tunnel walls might magnify sound, sending whispers for miles. Then you hear the sound of soft, shuffling footsteps ahead. It sounds like a large party.

Ten yards in front of you, the tunnel veers to the left. Torchlight flickers on the walls, casting ghostly shadows from around the bend. You shield your eyes from the sudden glare.

You look for a cross tunnel, anyplace to hide, but see nothing except solid stone.

"Not that way," someone says.

"Why not?" says a second voice.

"Because it leads back the way we came," the first voice replies.

Chain mail jingles loudly. A sword clangs against the side of the tunnel. You flatten yourself against the stone wall. How could the orcs have gotten ahead of you? Did you miss a side tunnel in the dim light?

"Are you sure?" another voice, a woman's, asks. "I don't think you have any idea where we are."

You take a deep breath and inch forward silently. At the bend, you peer around the corner.

A sigh of relief escapes you. It's a group of fighters from the tower. Renda, the archer, is in the lead beside her twin brother, Relf. Two others follow, a broad-shouldered man carrying a battle-axe and another with a flail. Others trail along behind.

They're all breathing hard, as if they've been running. "Hey, did you hear something?" Renda says.

"It sounded like it was just ahead of us," the one with the flail says. "But the last orcs we saw were back the other direction," says the one with the battle-axe.

You sheathe your sword quickly and step around the corner, holding your empty hands out in front of you. "Need some help?" you ask.

The group turns to face you. Relf and Renda both instinctively grab for their bows. The others stand there, stunned. Then Renda smiles in recognition, shaking her head, her coppery hair fiery in the torchlight. The others laugh nervously, releasing the tension. They rush forward to clap you on the back.

"We thought you were dead," Renda says, and the rest of them echo her words.

"So did I," you say. "At least now we're all stuck here in these tunnels together."

Turn to 37.

5

Despite your fatigue, you find you can't sleep. As the day brightens, you can't stop thinking about Fostyr, the battle in the forest around the tower, the Dragon's Eye under your tunic, and Tyrion's symbol, the raven's head, on Gorak's amulet.

If the dark sorcerer is indeed involved, you imagine ways to avenge Fostyr, the tower, and your father. But first you must get the eye safely to Crockport. You have a vital mission, and if you fail, then all those other sacrifices will have been wasted. The land of Iuz must not control the magic contained within the Dragon's Eye.

For a moment, you wish you had the magic skills to look into the eye and see how the others fared back at the tower. Resting fitfully in the bottom of the boat, Peri groans with suppressed pain, hissing with each breath. He seems to be weakening, and his wound from the arrow hasn't stopped bleeding.

Gentle swells ripple across the surface of Whyestil Lake, gurgling against the sides of the boat. The morning is quiet, and you can hear no sounds from the distant shoreline forests. They look fuzzy in the thin morning fog.

In the boat, Grigneth complains to himself, and Bresnor sits in grim, silent concentration as the two of them lean into the oars, slicing the water with even strokes. Each moment takes you closer to Crockport with your secret burden. Touching the heavy leather pouch beneath your jerkin, you finally let your eyelids close. At last you fall asleep to the hypnotic sound of the water lapping against the boat, with the dim sunlight of a thinly overcast day shining on your face. . . .

You wake suddenly. Frowning, you look around, trying to figure out what startled you. At your shoulder, Beatrix murmurs in her sleep, one arm pinned under her body; her face looks peaceful and vulnerable as she dreams. Grigneth and Bresnor continue to row with even, steady strokes. Vystan is quietly rummaging in the packs for something to eat.

You sit up. The normally choppy lake is clear and mirror-smooth, without a ripple. The breeze has died to a strange, stifling heaviness. You struggle to your knees, squinting into the still, green depths.

"Something's wrong . . ." you say.

A wheezy, gushing sound sighs over the boat, but doesn't disturb the water. You look up. In the boat's stern, Peri is fighting for breath. Vystan bends over him, wiping the blood from Peri's stomach with a strip of damp cloth. When the cloth is soaked with blood, Vystan holds it over the side of the boat and wrings out the rusty, pinkish water.

Beatrix sits up, also uneasy, shaking her long braid and fingering the dagger at her hip. Bresnor flicks his glance from side to side, suspicious.

You gaze across the lake at the trees bordering the shore. The morning mist has faded, but the lake remains still. You lean over the side to splash cool water on your face—just in time to see an immense dark shape drifting under the boat, only a few feet below the surface. You draw back, jarring the boat. Beatrix looks sharply at you.

Grigneth and Bresnor continue to row, unaware of the shadow. Vystan washes the bloody cloth again, dipping it over the side of the boat and leaving red swirls in the water. Below, the shadow eases slowly toward the stern.

You grip the gunwale with both hands. "Vystan," you say quietly, afraid the thing under the water will hear you. "Put the rag down. There's something following the boat."

Vystan turns, pulling the cloth out of the water, but it still drips into the lake. "What?" he says, looking puzzled.

"I'm not sure," you say, "but I think it's attracted by the blood."

Grigneth and Bresnor stop rowing. Bresnor's shoulders hunch as he peers over the side of the boat. Grigneth sighs with exhaustion and stretches his arms, more concerned with his aching muscles than any potential danger.

With a sudden splash, a glistening black behemoth rises out of the water next to Vystan, thrashing and hissing. Vystan gives a startled cry and jerks away, but the creature's pincers—the size and shape of blacksmith's tongs—close around his hand with a wet clack.

Vystan screams as the boat rocks to one side. Beatrix lunges to her feet, trying to keep her balance in the rocking boat. Bresnor grabs for his longbow. Grigneth huddles down in the bottom of the boat.

"Vystan! Let go of the rag!" you shout, scrambling over the others to reach him.

The portly man's pasty face is shiny with sweat as the mandibles of the monster squeeze down on his hand, keeping him from moving his fingers. "I'm . . . I'm trying!"

The creature rises out of the water, spitting spray from its mouth. Two huge, shiny black eyes glitter in the cloudy sunlight as beads of water run off its smooth, shiny carapace. The giant water beetle's club-like antennae thrash wildly along the sides of its neckless, human-sized head.

Vystan tries to wrench his hand away, but the beetle twists in the water, yanking him against the side of the boat. Long, jointed legs skitter against the wooden hull, pulling, trying to drag Vystan overboard into the lake.

"Help me!" Vystan cries.

Finally reaching him, you grab Vystan's breeches to keep him from being dragged over the side. The giant beetle's pincers scrape down his hand, tearing his flesh as they fasten on the bloody cloth. The cloth disappears into its clicking mandibles and dozens of moving mouth parts.

Vystan jerks his hand free, collapsing onto the bottom of the boat. Groaning, Peri tries to sit up and crawl away from the struggle.

With a quiet splash, the water beetle slips below the surface with its prize, a silvery bubble of air sheathing the underside of its body. With alternating kicks of its flat, reddish-black legs, it glides deep underwater and disappears.

"Take the oars!" you cry. "Let's get out of here before that thing comes back."

Beatrix shoves Grigneth aside to take one of the

oars. Bresnor grabs his oar, and together they begin to row furiously. Trembling, Vystan settles back onto his seat, holding his gashed hand and trying to fashion a bandage from another rag.

Peri groans and grasps the gunwale, pulling himself into a sitting position, moving toward the stern. The injured swordsman's wheezing becomes a ragged panting. He rests his head on the side of the boat.

Leaning over the side, you search the water for the giant beetle. Nothing. Everything is calm . . . too calm. As she rows, Beatrix scans the lake behind you. "What was that thing?" she asks.

"A giant water beetle," you say. "Every now and then they attack the fishing boats near Crockport."

"Can we kill it?" she asks, glancing meaningfully down at her lance. "I've had some experience spear-fishing."

"I don't know," you say. "Maybe it won't come back. It got what it wanted."

"We could always use Grigneth as bait," she mutters.

Grigneth tries to shrink down into the bottom of the boat.

You glance at Vystan, wondering if he'll be able to wield his flail with his injured hand. You reach for your own weapons. Your whip and oaken sword are useless against the beetle's armored shell. You pick up Bresnor's bow and nock an arrow, careful not to touch its metal tip. Maybe you can find a vulnerable spot if the thing rises out of the water again. Your greatest fear is that it will capsize the boat. You're far enough out that it may be difficult to reach the shore.

You whirl at a startling, retching sound at the far end of the boat. Groaning, Peri coughs blood. It splashes over the gunwale and into the water. "Peri!" you shout. "Cover your mouth!"

Peri slumps to the side, his head lolling over the gunwale so far that his black mustache nearly dangles in the water. Before anyone can reach the injured

man's side, the giant beetle surges out of the water, its pincers gripping Peri's head. Long, sharp legs reach over the gunwale, grab Peri's shoulders, and lunge backward. The weight of the beetle drags him over the side of the boat. Without uttering a sound, Peri disappears beneath the frothy pink water.

Stunned, you stare at the bubbles rising from the murky depths. Grigneth screams. No one else says a word. You hold your breath, waiting. Soon something pale and sacklike floats to the surface, a shriveled package wrapped in shredded clothes, little more than Peri's skin.

"By the gods!" Vystan whispers. "What happened?"

Beatrix's knuckles whiten around her lance. "It sucked him dry, that's what."

A choking sound escapes Grigneth. He sputters, then swallows. Bresnor shivers.

"Can we kill it?" Vystan says. Beatrix stands up and takes her lance, ready to skewer the beast as soon as it rises again. Deep below the boat, the dark shape continues to circle.

"I'm not sure," you say. "It might be better to try to outrun it. If it's attracted to spilled blood—"

"Here it comes again!"

Bresnor shouts, pointing.

Twenty yards away, a black shadow closes in on your boat. Beatrix and Vystan turn to you. "Well?" Vystan says. "Do we fight or try to outrun it?"

If you decide to fight the water beetle, turn to 30.

If you prefer to try to outrun it, turn to 38.

6

"Back away from the horgar . . . carefully," you say as you begin to inch backward. You motion for your companions to lower their weapons. "The risk is too great. I don't see any way we can kill it."

Renda, still looking terrified, nods in reluctant agreement. "Its skin is as hard as rock," she says. "I've never heard of anyone killing one of those things."

"You heard her," you say. "No heroes. Everybody keep his distance. Don't provoke it."

Relf looks out at you helplessly from behind the creature's massive body. It could crush him at any second.

Renda calls out, "Don't move, Relf!"

Her twin nods. "I don't think I'm going anywhere." He freezes as the horgar oozes toward him.

You and your companions continue to back away slowly toward the cave entrance, afraid to make any sudden movement. The horgar shifts uneasily, rumbling. Relf swallows and presses tighter against the wall. Silently you pray that the creature will ignore him. You can feel the veins in your temples throbbing.

The horgar raises itself slightly. Relf huddles against the cave wall.

"It's going to kill him if we don't do something," Renda cries, taking a step forward, grabbing for her bow.

You grab her arm. "If it wanted to kill him, it wouldn't have waited this long," you say softly.

Renda pauses, her muscles taut as a bowstring beneath your hand. Suddenly the horgar heaves its body toward the cave wall, blocking your view of Relf.

Renda gasps. "No!" she shrieks. She tears free of your grip and sprints back into the cave. You hear nothing from Relf.

You sprint after her, ordering the others to stay where they are.

The sluggish creature butts its head against the wall. You hear the rock hiss loudly, like water being tossed on a fire. The wall dissolves, and the horgar begins to slither forward into the newly created tunnel, chewing its way through the rock with its powerful acid.

As the last of the creature disappears into the tunnel, Relf runs to Renda.

You let out a sigh of relief. You clap Relf and Renda on their backs, then walk back to the others. "Let's try a different direction . . . okay?"

"You know, I got the feeling the horgar didn't really want to kill me," Relf says slowly. "I think it was just protecting itself. That's why it turned away when you left it alone."

You examine the horgar's original passage. It must have just tunneled in from somewhere when you first came upon it. You tell your companions to search the surrounding caves for another tunnel.

After a few minutes, Relf calls out, "I found it! Over here!"

You and your companions converge toward his waving torch. Relf stands at the opening to another smooth tunnel. It slopes gently upward.

"The sides don't feel hot," Relf says. "Look." He puts his hand on the tunnel wall.

The smell of acid is faint. Only a few puddles spot the floor. You feel a slight draft in your hair. "This is an old tunnel," you say.

"I say we follow it," Renda urges. "The torches won't last much longer. We've got to find a way out."

"I agree," you say, fingering the Dragon's Eye. "We've got to get to Crockport."

You and your comrades enter the old horgar tunnel. The passage steepens gradually. Before long, you're all breathing hard. It wouldn't be so bad if you weren't already so tired and hungry. Your legs feel like lead weights. The muscles in your thighs and calves spasm with fatigue.

The others aren't managing much better. You call a rest at a level spot in the tunnel and plop down on the hard floor.

"How much farther can this passage go before it reaches the surface?" Relf asks.

Renda licks her lips. "I don't know. I didn't think

we were so deep underground."

"Neither did I," you say. "But I've lost all my sense of direction."

You heave yourself to your feet. Your whole body is stiff and your arms and legs are dead tired, but it won't get better until you can get some fresh air, good food, and cool water. Your head spinning, you put a hand against the wall to keep from falling.

With a loud cry of pain, you yank your hand away, your fingers burned. "Watch out for the walls," you say. "There seems to be more acid."

You raise your torch. But it's not acid. Instead, a vein of bright silver glimmers in the flickering light. It must be the metal that touched your skin.

"Do you think we're getting close to the mines?" Renda asks.

"Maybe," you say. "If we are, it can't be far to an exit. Those miners had to get in and out somehow."

You and your companions forge ahead with renewed energy. After a while, the tunnel levels out and the pace picks up.

A faint current of air brushes your face. The air smells dank but fresh, not as stale as it has been.

You hurry forward. "At last . . . at last," you mutter, looking for a glimmer of sunlight. But the tunnel leads into a cavern so large that you can't even see the other side. You stop, your stomach tightening. It's not a mine. Worse, you can't see where the tunnel exits from the cavern.

Your companions cluster in a tight knot around you. Renda sighs heavily. "It looks like it was a false hope. I guess there's nothing to do but start checking out these other tunnels," she says.

"It sure looks that way," you say. You follow the others across the cave as they fan out, peering into the small passages leading away from the grotto walls.

A few minutes later, a voice cries out, then falls silent. You and several others hurry toward the noise. Torches cluster around a large outcropping of stone where Relf stands alone, waving his hands.

"What happened?" you ask as you rush to the edge of a pit to join Relf.

Relf turns to you, his eyes wide in his pale face. "It's Renda . . . she's fallen into the pit," he says.

Turn to 16.

7

You clutch the eye hidden beneath your tunic. Many people have already died to keep the talisman away from the evil wizard's grasp. Now Fostyr will be among them.

With an aching heart, you slip back into the bushes with your companions and head away from the orc camp. Your path leads up a gradual slope to the crest of a low ridge.

You stumble, unable to concentrate on where you're going. Branches whip your face, as if punishing you or trying to yank you back. But you stagger ahead, trying to escape from the feeling that you are deserting Fostyr.

You tell yourself there was no way for you to save your friend. There were just too many orcs. And Gorak. And Tyrion. What could you have done alone, or even with the small group of fighters beside you? And could you really have asked all of them to risk their lives for one person, especially at the risk of losing the eye?

Behind you, you hear the orcs cry out, cheering and chanting. You can't keep yourself from turning around again. You force yourself to watch.

Through the branches, you can still see Fostyr flanked by the wizard and the orog. Time seems to click into slow motion. Fostyr holds his head up high, confident that he has accomplished his mission.

You want to close your eyes, but you can't. You

stare at the scene in horror.

Gorak's muscles ripple as the orog puts all of its strength behind the axe blow, swinging it downward. Fostyr doesn't even cry out. He dies in silence.

The orcs scream and cheer, dancing around their bonfire.

You jam a fist into your mouth and bite down on your knuckles to keep from crying out. Your knees go watery. You lean against the rough trunk of a tree. You keep telling yourself there's nothing you could have done. Nothing you could have done . . .

Your companions come back to get you, supporting you as they retreat. They move off through the forest, away from the burning lights of the orc camp and to safety.

"There was nothing we could do," your companions tell you. You barely hear them. "We must live to fight another day."

You swallow and nod, finally able to walk unaided again. The wind blows cold through the trees.

Ahead of you, one of your companions shouts. You jerk your head up. "What is it?" you ask, one hand reaching automatically for your wooden sword.

"Look!" someone shouts. "Some of the others must have made it out of the tower!"

You quicken your pace. Soon the armed group appears, ten fighters in all. As they draw near, you recognize a thin man with a goatee, a minister of Count Delwyn's named Fabius. Now, however, he is wearing full armor and leading an escort of fighters.

Fabius approaches your party slowly, two burly soldiers at his shoulders. "We're looking for some friends," Fabius says.

"Which friends?" you ask.

Fabius narrows his eyes. You can sense he is trying to decide what to tell you, and how much. "The ones who were supposed to meet Count Delwyn. We know of your mission. If you still have the eye, we will escort you to safety."

"I have it," you say, but you feel no enthusiasm for the end of your quest. Not after seeing Fostyr's death.

You pull out the pouch with the eye and tug the strings binding the opening. You lift up the pearly sphere. Your companions gasp. Fabius reaches for the pouch, but you shake your head. "I have orders to give it to the count myself," you say.

Fabius considers this. "Fair enough," he says. "Follow us."

You nod, relieved. "We can use the help. Enough of us have died at Tyrion's hands. Too many."

As you walk, you forge a vow of vengeance. You failed this time, but you know your chance will come again. You swear to make the orcs and Tyrion pay dearly for Fostyr's death.

Someday you will fight them again—and next time, you will win.

The End

8

"Go, Corlen!" Fostyr says. "Into the tunnel!"

You hesitate in front of the dark opening, unwilling to leave your friend to certain death. The last of the defenders squeeze past you, scrambling down the stairs. If you don't go with them now, it will be too late.

"Save the eye," Fostyr urges. "If you don't, everything we've done here means nothing."

You grit your teeth. "Fostyr, I can't—"

"Stop arguing! I'll follow when I can."

Seven orcs leap from the stones in front of him. Their lips curl into snarls as they advance. Before you can react, Fostyr lets out a fierce battle cry. He rushes the orcs. Within seconds, they swarm over him, and he is lost in a flurry of swords and clubs. Other orcs advance toward you, blocking Fostyr from view.

Your heart stops, then races. There's nothing you

can do now except avenge Fostyr—and keep the Dragon's Eye safe.

An orc with a cat-o'-nine-tails jumps from the crumbling walls and lunges at you. You parry its attack, using its own momentum to force it to one side, bowling down two others. Without a glance behind you, you turn and leap down the steps after the rest of the party.

Three orcs follow you to the stairs. Their breathing rasps against the stone walls, the clank of their swords echoing in your ears.

"Hurry, Corlen!" someone shouts ahead of you. In the blackness, you can make out the edge of a heavy door lit from behind by torches. You take the remaining stairs three at a time. At the last second the door creaks open, and you stumble through, falling to one knee before catching your balance.

An orc's shrill scream pierces the air. The hair on the back of your neck prickles as the door clangs shut. One of the orcs slams into it, then smashes at the door with its battle-axe. But bronze-haired Relf slams a heavy crossbar in place.

Renda shrugs her bow higher on her shoulder, then grasps you by one arm. "Where's Fostyr?" she demands.

You shake your head.

"I'm sorry," she says. "I know he was your best friend." She helps you to your feet.

"Thanks," you say.

Relf thumps the side of his fist against the heavy door. You can hear orcs pounding on the opposite side. "That door won't hold them for long, but we can at least get a head start." Relf slips off one of the two quivers on his shoulder and hands it to you. "Here . . . you may need this."

The last of the tower defenders gather around you. Beside you stands a broad-shouldered man with a battle-axe. Another big man, Turloc, slouches next to him, a flail dangling in his hand. Several others mass behind them. Ten torches flicker in the dark, enough to last a few days if you burn only one at a time.

The door splinters and shudders behind you as more of the orcs begin to hack at it with their axes. You estimate five minutes, ten at the most, before the enemy soldiers break through the door.

"Where to?" someone asks, glancing warily at the door as if expecting it to shatter at any moment.

"We've got to get to a place we can defend easily," you say. "We'd better get moving." A murmur of assent rises from the group.

You take the lead down the corridor. Relf grabs a torch from one of the others and walks beside you. Renda follows a few steps behind, mirroring her twin's moves. You order the flail wielder and the soldier with the battle-axe to guard the rear.

After several minutes, you come to an intersection where four corridors come together. Good, you think, sticking to the main one. The orcs will have to guess which one you followed. Fostyr knew these tunnels well and would have known exactly where to go, but he can't help you now.

A pang of loss swells your throat. You swallow, forcing yourself to concentrate. You can worry about avenging his death later. For now, you have to get away with the eye.

The tunnel winds through several bends before it finally straightens out. You can well imagine that the Dragon's Eye could have been lost for centuries.

Your party passes two doors, both of them locked. After another few minutes, you see a third door, larger than the other two.

You approach it cautiously, ears straining for any sound, but you hear nothing beyond it. You try the handle. This door is unlocked. Renda and several others stand ready behind you. You take a deep breath, then pull on the handle.

The door opens into what looks like an empty room, with another door on the opposite side. You pause in the doorway.

"What's wrong?" Turloc asks. "What's in there?"

"Be quiet," you answer, peering into the room. The light from Relf's torch flickers on the walls, illuminating designs carved into the stone. On closer look, you see that they are bas relief sculptures of gods in human form. A semicircular dais sticks out from each wall, beneath the image of each god. A place to kneel and pray. You've never seen this place before. It smells of dust and decay.

You cross the room and open the second door. It leads into a straight corridor, identical to the one behind you.

The room looks like a good place to face the orcs, with only one way in and one way out. They won't be able to outflank you, and you can retreat if necessary.

"We'll set up here," you announce. "We have a clear shot down the corridor with our bows, and only one orc can attack at a time through that door."

Five minutes later, everyone is in position, waiting tensely. You station Turloc and the soldier with the battle-axe at the second door in case the orcs find their way around and to cover your retreat should it become necessary. Everyone has weapons held ready.

"Wait . . . I heard something," Renda says. She points to the chiseled bas relief sculpture next to the axe wielder. "A scratching sound . . . it sounded like it came from that wall over there."

With a flickering motion, the carved image of the god begins to move, pushing and struggling as it emerges from the wall, taking on three-dimensional form. Slowly it steps out onto the dais, looking down at the intruders.

Turloc stumbles back in fear and surprise, his flail raised and his eyes as big as plates. The stone god slowly rotates its head, then takes a step toward the axe wielder. The soldier feints to one side, then ducks in, swinging hard. The metal axe *chings* off the stone but causes no damage. In a motion too quick to see, the statue tears the axe from the man's hands. Thrown

off balance, the soldier trips and falls.

You rush forward, grabbing your whip. If you can tangle up one of the god's legs or arms, maybe you can pull it off balance.

Before you get a chance, the flail wielder darts in. His metal flail clangs loudly off the statue's stone arm. The god catches the next blow with one hand. Gripping the flail's iron chains, it yanks Turloc to the floor at its feet. It clenches its free hand and raises it like a boulder, ready to pound its victim flat.

"No!" Turloc cries, lifting his hands to protect his face. He ceases his struggles.

The fist freezes, and the stone god turns to look for another target, leaving the flail wielder cowering on the floor. A rock catches the deity in the side of the head and glances off. Relf pales, his fingers trembling around more rocks gathered from the floor of the chamber. The stone god turns to face him.

It moves surprisingly quickly this time, ignoring the rest of the group. Renda pushes her twin brother aside. Relf drops his rocks, and the stone god ignores him, turning its attention to Renda. She stands with her bow drawn, determination creasing her brow.

"Don't shoot, Renda," you shout. "If you hold your fire, it won't attack!"

Renda stands rigid, her bow drawn. At any second, you expect her to let the arrow fly, goading the god to kill the bronze-haired archer.

But she resists her impulse to shoot. The stone god stops in its tracks, waiting.

"Stand still," you order the others. "Don't do anything to threaten it. That's what makes it attack."

You lower your whip to your side. The rest of your companions do the same with their weapons. You can hear your heart hammering. You hope you've guessed right.

The god raises the hand clutching Turloc's flail, then drops the weapon to the ground, where it clangs hollowly on the stone floor. "Go," the god says. "Do not come back until there is no hatred in your hearts."

"Let's get out of here," you hiss. Turloc grabs his flail and hurries for the exit. You follow out the far door behind them. Renda waits for you.

"I don't think we have to worry about any orcs that enter *that* room," she says with a grim smile. "They'll never get out alive."

"Let's hope so," you say, wishing that the same tactic that worked with the stone sculpture would work with the orcs. But you know it won't happen. You and Renda hurry to catch up with the others.

Go to 37.

9

The murky Vesve Forest absorbs the tumult of the clash behind you. The thick white oaks and fragrant laurel trees smother the battle cries of orcs and humans. Your companions are uneasy, no doubt thinking thoughts similar to your own—that you have left the others at the tower to their fates, while you flee into the forest like cowards. But you must believe your mission is important, too. You and your companions must take the Dragon's Eye to safety.

Beside you, Beatrix's horse switches its tail, its ears folded back. Beatrix calms the beast with a soft shushing sound. When he hears it, Peri turns and glares at her. Your party proceeds with great care deeper into the forest beneath the thick, folded tree branches, wary of wide-ranging orc patrols. The forces of Iuz may well anticipate your band's mission, and you must be ready for anything.

Your horse is as skittish as Beatrix's, pulling at the bit and blowing softly. Its ears flatten and it backs up a few steps.

"Do you think the horses can smell the orcs?" you ask.

"Maybe," Peri says, scowling. His black mustache dances on his upper lip as he talks. "That's why we have to be quiet."

Fostyr glances around, looking up as a group of night birds stirs in the branches overhead. You peer between the nearby trees but see nothing. No one dares ignite a torch to light the way through the darkened woods.

Pressing your knees into your horse's ribs, you coax the animal forward. Off to your left, a tangle of brambles shivers, rustling like a hissing snake. A swooping sound fans the air. You clamp your mouth shut to keep from crying out. An owl rises with a field mouse in its talons. Only an owl, you tell yourself. Only an owl. You are the leader here, and you must keep up a brave front.

The quiet deepens around you.

"Nothing to worry about," Fostyr whispers.

Suddenly Bresnor shouts behind you as a fully armed orc scout crashes out of the underbrush in front of the horses. Sweat sheens its pitted green face. Its red eyes gleam, and its jumbled teeth gnash together as it hoists its battle-axe.

Everyone moves at once, drawing their weapons. Twisting in your saddle, you unsling your bow and nock an arrow. Before you can shoot, however, blonde-haired Beatrix, nearest the orc, runs the monster through with her lance. Then, with a heave from her strong biceps, she flings the body aside. Beatrix yanks her lance free and tosses her long braid over her shoulder. She looks at the rest of the party smugly. "That was easy enough," she says.

With an ear-piercing cry, another orc leaps from behind an oak tree in front of you, its rusty-toothed flail raised. Without a second's hesitation, you draw back your bowstring and let fly. The orc crumples to the ground, clutching the arrow in its neck.

A thick black arrow whistles over your shoulder, just missing your ear. You hear someone groan and collapse beside you. With a surly expression, Bresnor lowers his bow. You whirl to look down at a third orc sprawled on its back amid a tangle of brambles, its pike fallen to the ground beside it.

"Thanks, Bresnor . . ."

Shouts ring through the trees, drawing nearer. Then the shouts suddenly stop. The silence is eerie.

"We'd better get out of here fast," you say, nocking another arrow. "We need to put some distance between us and the tower."

Fostyr and Peri, with Bresnor between them, search the surrounding forest. Grigneth sits hunched on his horse, his hands twisting the reins, his leather helmet crammed down on his head. He scratches the reddish stubble on his chin.

As you wait, you peer into the shadows. A twig snaps somewhere off to the right, and you draw your bow, waiting for more orcs to appear. A doe steps from the copse, freezes, then bounds away.

You let out your breath, wiping sweat from your forehead. Your heart hammers in your chest. You've got to get the eye out of here or all is lost.

You glance at Grigneth. During the attack, Grigneth didn't draw his sword at all. You're concerned that he may have a hidden streak of cowardice. You decide to watch him closely. Perhaps you should carry the eye yourself, but you doubt Grigneth would give it to you willingly.

Grigneth fingers the leather thong around his neck. The pouch bobs up from under his jerkin. He releases the pouch, and it disappears again.

With the sound of cracking underbrush, Fostyr, Peri, and Bresnor return, their eyes flashing. "Orcs all over the place," Peri says, tugging on his mustache.

"Too many for us to fight," Bresnor adds, shifting his longbow behind him.

"We've found a few alternatives, though," Fostyr says. "We're not far from the lake." He points off through the forest. "There's a boat docked at the end of an old wharf. If we get to the boat, we can get to Crockport by water."

"Another possibility is a cave nearby," Bresnor pipes up. "It probably connects to the tunnels beneath the tower. You can see it from the pier."

"Good thinking," you say. You take a deep breath. "But we aren't trying to get back to the tower. We have to deliver the eye. Let's head for the boat." You look at Bresnor. "If we can't make it to the boat, we'll head for the cave."

Everyone nods. You take the lead and wind your way through the trees. Fostyr stays close to Grigneth, who mutters to himself and keeps fondling the eye beneath his leather breastplate.

Meanwhile you scan the woods around you. The continued silence of the orcs unnerves you. Where are they, anyway? They must know you're here. What are they planning? You tense every time a twig snaps or a bush rustles.

Finally you can see the shimmer of the lake in the moonlight through the trees. You glance over your shoulder and nod to your companions. Everyone quickens the pace. As you approach the last stand of laurel, you spy the pier, made of rotted slats of wood balanced on old stump pilings driven out into the muck of the shallows. Tied to one of the pilings is a wooden boat, partially filled with scummy rainwater.

You'll have to leave the horses and most of your provisions behind, but the passage across the water will be much safer than creeping through the orc-infested forest. All you have to do is cross the gravelly beach under the cover of darkness as the orc army is busy beseiging the tower. Then you and your party can clamber into the boat and set off across the dark, choppy waters. Motioning to the others with one arm, you spur your horse forward.

Partially concealed by the drooping branches of a dead willow, a cave mouth yawns off to your left, a slash of deeper black in the steep bank of the lakeshore. Only as a last resort, you think. You might be able to lose the orcs in the winding tunnels, but that would only cost you time and get you no nearer to the end of your quest.

"Let's go," you say quietly, heading toward the pier. The rocky beach makes crackling sounds under your horse's hooves.

As you venture out into the open, a hideous war cry rends the air. Startled, you swivel in your saddle. Behind you, grinning orcs spill from the woods, swords and battle-axes gleaming, pikes held high. They've been waiting for you!

Shouting, the orcs fall on your companions. The orcs are too close for you to use your bow effectively. You uncoil the whip at your waist and turn to fight.

"We can handle them," Fostyr shouts with stoic humor. "There's only a couple dozen of them!"

"Good thing we've got the horses," Peri, the swordsman, grunts as he joins in the fray beside Beatrix and her deadly lance. "I know I advised against it," he says, killing a yelling orc with a wide sweep of his sword, "but you were right, Corlen. We'd be dead meat on foot."

You and Fostyr cluster around Grigneth and the Dragon's Eye as Fostyr's sword slices through the neck of the nearest orc. Moving away from the battle, Bresnor nocks an arrow, aiming at an orc swinging a flail studded with poison thorns. The air whistles as Bresnor releases the bowstring. The orc stumbles to the ground, its chest pierced by the arrow.

At Grigneth's flank, you engage two orcs at once, slicing long gashes across their pocked faces with the tip of your whip.

With a sweep of her lance, Beatrix guts the orc nearest her, then growls as an arrow grazes her thigh. Vystan crushes the skulls of two orcs with a circular sweep of his flail.

In a blur of motion, another orc hurls itself at you, its halberd raised high. With a crack of your braided leather whip, you flick the weapon from its hand, then lash out again. The whip coils tightly around the orc's neck, crushing its windpipe. Then, with a quick jerk of your wrist, you snap the creature's neck. Tugging the whip free, you urge your horse over the orc's body and deeper into the heart of the skirmish.

You crack your whip, nicking the hands of an orc archer aiming at Fostyr. The arrow is deflected off target, but it plunges deep into the heart of your friend's mount. Fostyr's horse stumbles, throwing him to the ground as more orcs swarm out of the forest, screaming battle cries.

You gallop toward Fostyr, grabbing his thin arm and easily pulling him up onto your horse in front of you. He clasps your horse's neck, panting, as you move past his own dying mount. "We've got to save Grigneth and the eye!" Fostyr exclaims.

You wheel your horse and charge back down the gravel beach. Small, broken stones fly out beneath the horse's hooves. You gallop between Grigneth's flank and an orc with a battle-axe. Fostyr lets loose of your horse's neck with one arm and uses his sword to lop off the orc's hand. Snapping out with your whip, you manage to disarm an orc archer, breaking his fingers with the stinging force of the blow. But more of the monsters continue to emerge from the trees.

In front of you, the enemy captain, an orog—a creature larger and meaner and more intelligent than the rest of the orcs in the ambush party—stands on the beach, bellowing, its purplish face knotted with hatred. "Get eye! Where is eye?"

One of the other orcs shouts, pointing at Grigneth. "Eye here, Gorak!"

The orog shouts a command to all of his soldiers to attack. Finding their target, the orcs swarm toward Grigneth. Beatrix, Peri, and Vystan rush to head them off. Bresnor urges his horse closer to Grigneth's, trying to get off a clear shot with his longbow.

You and Fostyr, already close to Grigneth, brace

for the onslaught. You clutch the oaken sword at your hip, drawing it. You curse the wizard Tyrion and the spell that forbids you to touch metal. Someday Tyrion will pay for that. And for your father's death.

If you live that long.

With Fostyr in front of you, you spur your mount forward to help Grigneth. Then you freeze. Around Gorak's neck hangs an amulet bearing a raven's head . . . the wizard Tyrion's symbol.

An orc leaps in front of you, screaming and waving its sword. Your horse rears unexpectedly. You grab the reins, accidentally wrapping your fingers around a metal buckle, which sears like fire into your knuckles. With a cry of pain, you tumble from the horse, landing on the bow strapped to your back. It snaps in two.

Fostyr struggles with the frightened horse but manages to get it under control. "Let's get Grigneth out of here," Fostyr shouts. "Head for the boat!"

Your quiver slips from your shoulder as you scramble onto Grigneth's horse in front of him. The flint-tipped arrows spill to the ground. Vystan, Peri, and Beatrix are already galloping for the boat.

"Get to the boat, Corlen! It's our only chance," Fostyr calls between gritted teeth.

"Come on!" Grigneth shouts in panic, grabbing your shoulders and trying to snatch the reins out of your burned fingers.

Fostyr swats the flank of Grigneth's horse with the flat of his blade. The startled horse races toward the lake. Peri gallops to join you; then Vystan and Beatrix bound from the trees. They flank Grigneth, shielding him from the orc arrows and spears.

You swing around to look. Fostyr hacks wildly with his sword, blocking a group of orcs trying to get past him to the beach, but he is only one against many. Several orcs outflank him and hurry after you, their short legs pumping furiously.

As you watch in horror, the huge orog captain pulls Fostyr from your horse and holds him aloft, like a trophy, in the air. "Get out of here!" Fostyr screams at you. "Save the eye!"

You turn to find that you have almost reached the dock. You yank the horse to a halt, skittering gravel on the rugged beach at the base of the pier.

Two orcs are only a short distance behind you, puffing and snarling as they run with their heavy weapons. Grigneth clambers down off his horse as the others pull their mounts to a stop. You start to slide out of the saddle just as the orcs hurl themselves at you. The taller orc thrusts with a short sword. The other swings at Grigneth with a mace.

Unconsciously Grigneth tries to dodge the mace, but the heavy weapon glances off his forearm, which begins to bleed freely. He grabs you desperately and pulls you to the ground with him. As you struggle to rise, he stuffs something down the neck of your jerkin. Your fingers brush against it. It's hard and cool and round . . . the pouch with the Dragon's Eye!

"This one has eye!" an orc shouts, grabbing Grigneth's shoulder. "Get him!"

You stagger to your feet, reaching for your whip. Grigneth leans forward, then draws his good arm back and smashes the orc's nose with a gloved fist, pulling away from its grip. "I don't have the eye, you fool!" Grigneth says. "He does!"

"Get to the boat!" Peri shouts, already out on the pier.

You start to run, then hesitate as more orcs rush toward Grigneth. He meets them with flailing arms and legs, a windmill of vicious kicks and punches. You aren't sure if he was being cowardly or giving you a chance to get away with the precious talisman.

Stout Vystan and blonde Beatrix charge past you to Grigneth's aid. Vystan twirls his flail over his head. He smashes it into the shoulder of the nearest orc, then raises the flail again. With her bloody lance, Beatrix skewers the other orc clinging to Grigneth.

You finger the whip, then withdraw your hand. The

eye rests like a heavy responsibility inside your jerkin. *That* is your primary mission. You've got to keep it from falling into Tyrion's hands! Suddenly you understand Grigneth's reluctance to fight.

You turn and run, but you're not sure which way to go. The way to the cave is clear, and you could make it there before the orcs realize what you're doing. You may be able to lose them in the tunnels.

Farther down the beach, a group of orcs is already swarming into the waters of Lake Whyestil, hoping to intercept the boat. You're not even sure the old vessel could carry your party. It looks as if it may split apart and sink the moment anyone jumps aboard.

Bresnor and Peri are already racing down the pier, motioning for you to follow. You start after them just as two more orcs rush toward you, cutting you off. You might be able to get to the boat, but you'll have to defeat both orcs, and by that time, a dozen more may be upon you. It might be safer to flee to the protection of the cave.

If you decide to head for the cave, go to 22.
If you elect to try to make it to the pier, turn to 21.

10

Weary, sore, and cautious, you and your party steal quietly through Vesve Forest. A light glimmers ahead of you through the rustling leaves and branches. You creep forward, reminding yourself that you are in hostile territory. No doubt a number of orc scouting parties are ranging even this far from Dragon's Eye Tower.

One of your companions in the lead stops and holds up his hand to caution the others.

You approach as quietly as you can, picking your way through vines and underbrush. You hear laughter ahead of you, a loud, coarse laughter that chills your blood, then the familiar rasp and snick of metal on stone. Someone ahead is sharpening a sword or an axe. An argument breaks out, followed by the sounds of a scuffle. The stink of roasting, spoiled food and the familiar reek of orcs sets your nerves on edge.

The other members of your party turn and look at each other. "Let's get out of here," someone says.

"I'm with him," says someone else. "If we stick around, we're as good as dead."

You hesitate. You know your party is in grave danger, yet you're curious about the orc camp at the same time. It would be useful to know how many orcs there are and if they're preparing to break camp. And that laugh. . . . But the Dragon's Eye tugs at you, reminding you of your first duty.

"All right," you say. "We'll go. Quiet, everyone."

You creep away, skirting the firelight. A branch cracks under your boot. You freeze, but the distant laughter gets louder. The orcs begin to cheer and shout. Something important must be going on. At least you don't have to worry about them hearing you over all the racket.

Suddenly a cry of pain pierces the air, a thin, exhausted voice . . . a familiar voice.

You pass by a small opening in the brambles and stop cold. You're closer than you thought from the edge of the orc camp, less than twenty yards in all. A group of orcs is playing dice nearby. A pock-marked orc draws its dagger, slobbering and cursing loudly, its red eyes flashing. The other orcs join in the argument.

"Keep moving," the flail wielder whispers through gritted teeth. "They won't see us."

You start to move on when the orc lowers its dagger and turns toward the main campfire. The other orcs do the same. As they turn, you can see past them briefly. You can't tear your gaze away.

"What is it?" a spearwoman asks, edging up behind you. "Guards?"

"No," you say, your voice tight. "It's my friend, Fostyr. He's still alive, and they've got him."

Fostyr stands a few yards beyond the group of orcs, his eyes glazed in the firelight. Looking emaciated, he sways unsteadily on his feet, ready to collapse. You swallow, anxious to do something but knowing your chances are virtually zero. His skin is pale, covered with dirt and bruises.

A purple-skinned orog steps forward and shoves Fostyr to his knees. You recognize Gorak. The orog's sickly colored hands are wrapped around a chipped but sharp battle-axe.

"Hurry," the pike carrier urges. "Before they see us."

You wave your hand to silence your companion just as a dark, charismatic man walks up next to Gorak. He seems to flow like shadows on his feet.

Your pulse quickens. "Tyrion!" you mutter, feeling your mouth become as dry as limestone.

The wizard stares at Fostyr, lips pinched and cruel as he smiles down at your wiry friend. The spell-engraved sword your father made for him hangs from Tyrion's hip.

The wizard unsheathes the sword. It shines with a reddish luminance in the flickering firelight, like copper . . . or blood. The runes your father etched into the steel still gleam brightly, potently. Your lip curls in a barely restrained snarl. Without those magical runes, Tyrion would lack any skill with a sword.

The laughter in the camp dies down. The orcs look expectantly at Tyrion.

"I'm tired of playing games," Tyrion says to Fostyr. "This is your last chance. Where is the Dragon's Eye?"

Fostyr lifts his chin. "I told you. It was taken to Crockport just before you destroyed the tower."

Tyrion shakes his head. "I have friends in Crockport. If the eye had been delivered to Count Delwyn, I would know about it."

"It's not there?" Fostyr says, visibly shaken.

Tyrion steps closer. "You really don't know, do you?"

Fostyr says nothing.

Tyrion steps back. "I'm convinced he knows nothing." He turns to the hulking orog beside him. "He's all yours."

The flail wielder leans close to you. "Enough of this, Corlen," he says. "We've waited long enough. We're going to get caught!"

"No," you say. "We've got to help Fostyr."

The spearwoman places a hand on your arm. "There's nothing we can do," she says. "They outnumber us six to one."

In the firelight, Gorak steps forward. The orog wets its lips and raises its huge battle-axe. Fostyr watches with wide eyes, but does not cringe.

You shrug her hand from your arm, torn by indecision. Above all, you need to protect the eye, and if you make any move now, you seem certain to be overwhelmed. Fostyr has already sacrificed himself once so you could save the eye. You'd never forgive yourself if the talisman fell into Tyrion's hands.

But at the same time, you would never forgive yourself if you stood by and let Fostyr die.

If you choose to flee with your companions, go to 7.

If you choose to try to rescue Fostyr, go to 29.

11

You decide to trust the second Count Delwyn, despite—or perhaps because of—his willingness to give up his sword only to you. Normally a count of the Kingdom of Furyondy would never hand over his weapon. But the fact that he is willing to part with it in this instance convinces you to trust him. It's not likely an important man such as the count knows about the curse that forbids you to touch metal. It wasn't something you spoke of openly after your father's death. Few people in Crockport know.

Besides, you *want* to believe the man who has found Fostyr, even if your friend seems to be trapped under a spell. Once you have gotten rid of the eye, you can take Fostyr to one of the magic-users in the city to cure your friend. Your other companions look at you uncertainly, but no one seems to have any better idea. Even the captain of the guards and his men eagerly watch the outcome of your decision.

"Count Delwyn, I offer you the Dragon's Eye," you say. Kneeling, you reach into the pouch and lift out the glasslike eye. It gazes coldly at you, feeling heavy in your hand. A chill runs up your spine, as if frigid power leaks out of its petrified depths.

The world seems to hold its breath. The wind picks up again, whipping the count's azure cloak so that it unfurls and snaps behind him. His sword remains drawn and extended out toward you, jeweled hilt first, inviting you to take it. You can see no expression at all in Delwyn's eyes. Fostyr stands immobile at the count's side, staring blankly past your right shoulder.

You spot a tiny flicker in your friend's eyes. Is it fear?

The count sheathes his sword and reluctantly lowers both hands, palms cupped, to receive the talisman. "Give it to me."

He snatches the eye and grips it tightly. A smile carves his lips as he stares into its night-black pupil. He whispers faintly, as if speaking into its dark depths.

" 'Two eyes from on high,' " the count intones. " 'One eye to see into the mind and heart. One eye to see the land below.' "

The ground begins to tremble. A shield with a coat of arms on the wall behind the count clatters to the courtyard. You back away, suddenly fearful of both

the Dragon's Eye and Count Delwyn.

"He's the sorcerer!" Beatrix shouts, realizing it even as you do.

As the false count raises the talisman level with his own gaze, he begins to shimmer. His azure cloak deepens to coal black. His face changes. His skin grows sallow, and his eyebrows thicken. His lips thin to a cruel line, pale and scarlike. His voice, once deep and resonant, fades to a scratchy whisper. The words gurgle in his throat, shrouded with phlegm.

You grow numb with despair, unable to move. Your arms and legs feel as heavy as iron.

"Thank you, dear Corlen," Tyrion rasps. "For the second time, you have failed miserably. When are you going to learn? You couldn't have helped me more if you were one of my own orogs."

Tyrion cackles, then bursts into a wreath of magical flame. You cry out, singed and blinded by the sorcerous flash. Everything around you vanishes into a red, blurry haze.

Slowly the haze clears, and you can see again.

"Search the castle!" the true count orders, shouting up to the guards on the battlements. "We have to find him. He has the Dragon's Eye!"

The captain hurries off with his guards. You sag to the ground, your face buried in your hands.

"Corlen, what happened?" The voice sounds familiar. Your heart leaps, and you look up. Fostyr stands beside you, the blank look gone from his eyes. Tyrion's spell is broken, now that he no longer has use for the captive young man. But the sorcerer himself has escaped—and the eye is gone.

Now that Tyrion and the eye are joined, no one in Furyondy can stand against them. You moan. What will the future bring? Terrible battles . . . tremendous grief. That much, at least, is certain.

The End

12

You decide to attack the horgar, hoping to distract it long enough for Relf to scamper to safety. You borrow a bow and arrows from a companion.

"Attack from all sides," you say. "We don't know how to kill it, but we'll never know if we don't try."

You motion for your companions to fan out around the enormous creature of liquid rock. The acid heat rising from the beast flushes your face. The air around it shimmers.

Renda nocks an arrow and takes aim. "Relf . . . duck!" she calls. Her arrow skitters harmlessly off the horgar's back, its tip shattered. The arrow bursts into flame as it grazes the rocky skin.

The horgar inches closer to the bronze-haired archer, making it more difficult for anyone to hit the creature without hitting Relf, too.

"Does the horgar have any weak spots?" you ask Renda.

She shakes her head. "Its skin is supposed to be as hard as rock. I've never heard of anybody killing one." She nocks another arrow and takes aim grimly along its shaft. "But there's always a first time."

"We don't need to kill it," you say. "We just need to get it to back off."

"Enough talk," says a burly, bald man with a huge battle-axe. He hefts his weapon and lunges forward with a yell, striking the horgar's stony side. The curved blade clangs, twisting in the man's hands.

The horgar turns more quickly than you could imagine possible for such an enormous creature. The bald man steps back, his axe raised for another blow at what looks like the horgar's boulder-shaped head.

A stream of acid squirts from the creature, catching the man full in the face. He screams, dropping his axe, and stumbles away, both hands covering his eyes.

"I can't see!" he screams, collapsing to the floor. His head smokes and sizzles.

You and Turloc rush to his side, but there's nothing you can do. As you watch helplessly, the skin dissolves away down to his skull.

A woman behind the horgar throws her spear. It ricochets off, bouncing to the floor. Turloc leaps to his feet and darts in with his flail. He slams the beast with the jangling, flexible chains, then hastily retreats. The horgar turns its back to Relf, but the young archer still has no room to get past.

"Arrows and spears only," you say. "Aim for its head . . . that lumpy part on top."

There must be an opening somewhere, something vulnerable . . . a mouth or eyes or soft underbelly. But you can't imagine how to hurt a creature made of solid rock.

A volley of arrows clatters off the horgar's steaming hide. They drop to the floor, their shafts in flames, flickering like candles in the dim cave.

"Relf, just hold on!" Renda cries in an attempt to comfort her twin.

Another spray of acid arcs from the horgar's head. Another man shrieks. He limps out of the firelight, clutching his leg, where the skin smokes and bubbles.

You pull back your bowstring and shoot. The arrow strikes the spot where you saw the acid spray from. It lodges for a moment, then bursts into flames.

The horgar rears up, charging the woman who threw the first spear. She leaps aside, diving to the floor and rolling to avoid another spray of acid. Her face contorts with pain. She wipes her left hand on her tunic. Sweat pours down her chalk-white face as, aghast, she watches her hand begin to sizzle.

"Now, Relf! Run!" Renda yells at her brother. She nocks another arrow.

Relf darts past the horgar as the beast goes after the spearwoman on the floor. The woman scoots to the wall, pressing herself against the stone, ignoring her burned hand.

Another fighter with a sword slips behind the horgar. He raises the sword and plunges the tip of the blade into a crevice in the rocky skin. Sparks shoot from the metal.

The horgar twists in a fluid motion. The man leaps to one side, but the horgar catches him in the hip. A scream of agony escapes from the man as his leather breeches burst into flame. As the man tries to smother his burning clothes, the horgar sprays him with acid. The man gurgles once, then collapses.

"Renda," you call. You point toward the monster's head. She nods. You both shoot at the same time. The arrows bury themselves in the horgar's rocky snout. Their shafts immediately catch fire. The horgar rears up again, making a low, rumbling sound.

"Get back!" you shout, but the others are already retreating from the cave. "Let's get out of here."

Relf hurries to join you and Renda. You urge them ahead, bringing up the rear. You back out, keeping an eye on the horgar.

The creature lumbers toward you, then halts, refusing to follow farther. A few more steps and you breathe easier. At the release of tension, weariness floods your muscles. Your foot catches on a rock. You fall to your knees. Renda grabs you by one arm and helps you up.

You shake your head, mumbling an apology. You had no idea how tired you were. You limp after Renda, Relf, and the others, following them back to the huge cavern.

You take stock. Two dead and several wounded, burned by acid, and four torches lost, left behind in the mad rush to escape.

You give everyone a few minutes to catch his breath, then you clear your throat. "Let's get out of here," you say. "No telling what else might be coming after us."

Turn to 27.

13

You ignore the stranger, but his appearance disturbs you. Suddenly sober, you say to your companions, "I think we should get out of here."

"What?" Vystan asks, his mouth stuffed from another helping of stew. He looks sadly at his bowl.

Bresnor and Beatrix both sit up straight, suddenly alert, and glance around at the crowd.

"Too many people are watching us," you say. "The sooner we get the eye delivered to Count Delwyn, the better."

You stand, stretching your aching legs. You would love to wash up, change into fresh clothes, and sleep in a warm, comfortable bed. But you cannot stop yet.

You look around, but the suspicious stranger has vanished. "Come on," you say, leading the others to the door.

The innkeeper bustles in from the back room and looks at the food remaining on your table. "We'll be back!" Vystan calls. "Make some more of that stew!"

As your group emerges from the Rusty Fishhook into the narrow streets, you look around again, but no one is in sight. Overhead, the moon is a bright eye, shadowed by clouds.

"Where are we going?" Beatrix asks, holding her lance at her side.

"To Count Delwyn's castle," you say. "Once we deliver the eye, we can take a well-deserved rest."

"That's for sure!" Grigneth says. You, Bresnor, and Beatrix all glare at him.

You hurry through the streets. Beatrix, Vystan, and Bresnor walk beside you, while Grigneth lags behind, complaining and limping on his wounded leg.

You know these streets well, and you grow more confident as you lead your companions through back roads to the southern outskirts of Crockport. It's long past midnight, and the town is quiet, sleeping. The streets become deserted as the flickering torchlights at intersections burn low. Even the night creatures have gone back to their dens to doze in the deep stillness.

Moving with a strange hush, you cross a stone bridge over a canal leading to Lake Whyestil, then stop at a steep path that winds its way uphill to the fortified castle of Count Delwyn.

As a child, you never ventured up the path to the castle, knowing that the noble's guards would keep beggars and curiosity seekers away. Now you must proceed. Your quest is nearly over.

"It'll be good to get inside," Grigneth says, slapping his arms against the evening chill. "Maybe he'll provide quarters for a few days. I could sure use a rest."

Beatrix looks up at the tall structure. "Another flagon of ale would sit well, too."

"Not to mention breakfast," Vystan adds.

"Well," you say, "what are we waiting for?"

You begin trudging up the cobblestone path. Long ago, Count Delwyn's father enlisted large work crews to pave the entire road up to the castle. The path switches back sharply for a distance, then breaks through the trees that line the hillside and levels out slightly, angling up the craggy face of the mountain.

As you ascend, the wind picks up, blowing the clouds across the moon, which is about to set on the western horizon. The cold breeze howls in your ears like a living thing, chilling you to the bone. You wrap your cloak around you more tightly. So do the others.

"Why would anyone want to live way up here?" Grigneth complains, huffing laboriously. The wind nearly carries away his words.

"It's easy to defend," Bresnor answers him.

"Count Delwyn doesn't trust anyone," you add. "He's afraid someone will rob him, so he lives where an army of trusted soldiers can guard him."

"Delwyn doesn't need any soldiers," Vystan mutters, looking up at the forbidding walls of the fortress, shadowed in the predawn darkness. "An enemy would be half dead from this hike by the time he got to the count's gates. Whew!"

Beatrix claps him on the shoulder. "You can die here if you want, Vystan," she says. "We'll pick you up on the way down."

"Thanks," Vystan says. The others chuckle.

The five of you pause beneath a rock outcropping, sheltered from the wind. Huddling close, you rest for a few minutes, then trudge onward, anxious to get to the mountain's summit and Count Delwyn's castle.

"We're almost there," you say, as if trying to convince yourself. The wind grows stronger as you approach the summit. Your cloak flaps up around you like a banner.

Finally the walls of Count Delwyn's castle loom before you, ancient stones weathered a deep gray-black and splotched with lichen and moss. A guard above the portcullis shouts a warning as you approach.

A handful of Delwyn's guards appear beside the crenellations of the wall to draw their longbows and nock arrows.

"Identify yourselves," the captain of the guard booms over the howl of the wind. His gray leather armor is the same color as the stones behind him. It's hard to see him in the fading moonlight.

You walk forward, arms spread wide. "My name is Corlen. We're on a mission from Dragon's Eye Tower," you shout back. "My father was Corrh, the swordmaker, once well known in these parts."

"Your father was known far beyond Crockport. What do you want?" asks the captain.

"We need to see Count Delwyn. He's expecting us. We have something to deliver to him."

"The count is ill. He can't see anyone."

"Captain Jongh at Dragon's Eye Tower told me to deliver my package to no one but the count," you insist. "We've had a difficult journey, and the fate of the land could depend on the success of our mission. We must deliver this into his safekeeping."

You pull the pouch from under your jerkin and hold it out so that the captain of the guard can see it. His archers lower their bows. "What is that, a bribe?" shouts the captain. "I see a pouch, nothing more."

Realizing that you must convince him of the importance of your quest, you reluctantly loosen the pouch's drawstring and carefully remove the Dragon's Eye. The pupil of the petrified eye gleams in the torchlight shining down from the battlements as if it's still alive. You turn it toward the captain.

A gasp escapes the guards. Their bows waver. Even the captain is visibly awed.

"By the gods," he says, "it's the Dragon's Eye! I'll be down in a minute to take it to the count."

"Our orders are to give it to Count Delwyn," you repeat. "I'm sorry, but I must hand it to him myself."

The captain grunts. "Fair enough," he says. "Wait here while I go summon the count. Maybe this'll lighten his black mood."

"Or maybe it'll make him even more uneasy," Bresnor mutters sourly.

Your hand trembles as you replace the eye in its pouch, glad to be out from under its cold gaze. You clutch the sack in your hand tightly.

Minutes later, the captain of the guard returns. "Count Delwyn has agreed to give you an audience. Keep your weapons sheathed, or you'll find out how good my archers are." He turns to one of the guards. "Go on, let them in."

With a loud groan and the creak of metal against metal, the guards draw up the heavy portcullis. You lead your band beneath it, glancing up nervously at the gate's hanging iron spikes as you enter the forbidding castle of Count Delwyn.

Go to 41.

14

By the time you reach the courtyard, the orcs are swarming toward a breach in the earthen wall where the giant sorcerous fist tore a wide section away. Dragon's Eye Tower is a pile of rubble. Rock dust billows in the air, accompanied by the last echoes of the tower's collapse. You know many fighters lost their lives in the wreckage. You look around for Fostyr and find him standing dazed, his face smeared with dust.

"Fostyr!" you shout, and your voice seems to make him wake up. He rushes to your side as the screeching orc fighters pour through the shattered perimeter walls.

Torches sputter all around you in the courtyard. Combined with the light of the moon, it is bright enough to see what you are fighting.

"Archers, find a high position and fire at will," Captain Jongh shouts over the orcs' screams. "Everyone else with me. We've got to mount our ground defense."

You turn to Fostyr. He nods for you to join the remaining archers, then draws his own sword. You are uneasy to be separated from your friend, but now isn't the time to worry about such things. You must defend what's left of the fortress. Fostyr sprints after Captain Jongh to seal off the gap in the earthen wall.

You scramble to the top of the perimeter wall near the breach. Though orcs pour through into the courtyard, the actual gap is narrow, easily defensible from above with enough archers, backed by a regimented squadron of brave fighters below.

You glance off into the distance, foolishly hoping to see the army of reinforcements from Crockport arriving just in time to save the day, but of course there hasn't been enough time, and only an overwhelming force of orcs awaits out in the forest.

You nock an arrow and shoot, sending a spear-wielding orc flapping backward off a pile of stones. The next arrow drops an orc carrying a huge battle-axe. You shoot rapidly, with your arm continuously moving back to your quiver, then to your bowstring. Time seems to slow down. The sounds of wounded orcs and humans, the buzzing of bowstrings, and the clash of blades and armor all combines into a deafening roar.

Your focus is sharp. You can see where each arrow is going to strike before it leaves your bow. Despite the din around you, the only sound you pay attention to is the beating of your heart.

Twenty arrows later, your quiver is empty, and time clicks back to normal. You feel helpless as the battle suddenly accelerates, bringing with it cries of pain and short-lived triumphs, and the clang of metal.

The orcs surround the walls, swarming like vicious ants. Several teams carry makeshift ladders, rushing through the swirling orc soldiers to lean the ladders against the walls. You search the courtyard below, looking for Fostyr, but see only turmoil as the fighters try to defend against the orcs that have managed to slip through the breach. The top of the wall is a mass of confusion, too. Bodies litter the ramparts.

Without any more arrows, you sling the bow over your shoulder. Unfastening your whip, you make your way to a point along the wall where one of the rickety orc ladders has just been raised. The ladder sways and dips as a dozen orcs try to scale the rungs. One orc reaches the top, sword uplifted to ward off the thrust of a spear from one of your comrades. The orc's face is exposed, red eyes glaring as if they have been boiled in blood.

Your whip cracks, too fast to be seen in the darkness, and a cut opens on the orc's face, slicing across one eye. The orc screams in surprise. Raising a hand to the bloody gash, it topples from the ladder, knocking off three of its comrades on the rungs, until it crashes into the packed enemy army below.

You move on to your next target, another troop of orcs scrambling up a ladder. The heads of the orcs are close enough that you can reach most of them from above with your whip. But there are too many ladders and not enough defenders. You wish you had another few caldrons of that boiling oil.

At a dozen other points, the orcs gain the top of the wall, forcing your comrades into tiny knots. You fasten your whip to your belt, then draw your oaken sword. You join a small cluster of five defenders. Facing outward, you protect each other's backs.

By now your arms ache, as exhaustion finally grows stronger than your excitement. Your lungs feel as if they are on fire, and each breath fans the flames in your chest. Sweat drips from your brow and stings your eyes until you can barely see. But still you continue to fight.

The metal tip of an orc spear catches you in the cheek. The reaction of the curse makes your face feel as if you have laid it down on burning coals. But there is no blood, since Tyrion's curse cauterizes the wound before it can bleed.

More and more blades slash at you. One of your companions falls dead beside you. You fight furiously, the sting of naked metal causing painful injuries from even glancing blows. Before long, the air around you is tainted with the stench of burned flesh, and charred cuts cover your hands and arms. Your oaken sword is no match for most of the orc weapons, and your only chance is to go for their exposed eyes and throats.

The orcs force your group off the wall and down into the rubble-strewn courtyard in front of the collapsed tower. They push you toward the dwindling number of fighters still trying to defend the breach.

"Into the tunnels!" Fostyr shouts. "It's our only chance!"

Your heart leaps, buoyed by his voice. Then it sinks again at the sight of Captain Jongh's bloodstained body lying among the rubble. His nose has been broken again by the same mace blow that killed him. The splintered shaft of a spear sticks out of his chest. Dead orcs litter the rubble around him, and you know he did not give up easily. You hope you can do half as well when your time comes.

With Captain Jongh dead, only you and Fostyr know where the real Dragon's Eye is. You must take the eye to safety and not let it fall into the hands of Tyrion. You realize with a sinking feeling that you should have fled long before now.

You look around wildly, searching the semidarkness for Fostyr. You have to get away.

Your friend stands among a pile of huge stones at the foot of what used to be the tower. A shadowy stairwell descends into black, musty passages nearby. He motions frantically for the others to follow him. Your remaining comrades are already battling their way toward the tunnels, including the twins Relf and Renda. A few stay behind to slow the progress of the orcs. A tall orc slashes at you viciously with a long sword. You duck, then leap from the pile of stones and sprint toward Fostyr.

Twenty feet from the passage, an orc carrying a huge gnarled club springs from behind a pile of debris into your path. Its tattered fur clothing reeks of rotting animal flesh. The creature grins at you, baring its decayed, broken fangs. Its fetid breath reeks of putrefying meat.

"No escape," it hisses, glaring at you. Its blood-red eyes make your skin crawl. It stalks toward you, club uplifted, ready to cave in your skull.

Holding up your useless wooden sword, you circle to your right, moving away from the rubble to avoid getting trapped. The orc angles to cut off your escape. You back up, thinking to climb the pile of stones just behind you and gain an advantage.

Before you can climb, the orc lunges, swinging at your head. You duck quickly, but a knot at the end of the club glances off your shoulder.

Even with your thick leather armor, the pain sucks your breath away. Your vision goes black for just a second, but you can't allow yourself to fall into unconsciousness. You sink to your knees, slashing blindly, hoping to catch the orc in the legs.

The blade deflects clumsily off something, and you hear a bellow as you try to swim back to consciousness. You throw yourself to one side and roll just as the spiked club whizzes past your head, brushing your face with air.

The orc stumbles and grunts as you come out of the roll into a squat. Dust billows around you. You blink from all the flying grit. Your vision clears in time to see the orc's face contort with rage.

It leaps at you, screaming. You back into a wall of solid stone that jabs you between the shoulder blades.

Then the orc is on top of you, clawing at your throat with its bare hands.

You twist to one side, swinging the attacker around. The orc's face slams into a jagged stone block with a grunt, leaving the back of its neck exposed.

You raise your oaken sword with both hands and swing the blade with all of your strength into its neck.

The impact rattles your hands and arms. You wince at the loud crack and stagger back, afraid that the wooden blade of your sword has split. But the polished oak sword proves to be stronger than the bones in the monster's neck.

The orc shudders, its spine crushed. It drops its club and crumples to the ground.

Sucking in huge lungfuls of air, you stagger away from the orc, running to the stairwell. Adrenaline dulls the pain in your shoulder. The Dragon's Eye feels very heavy on your chest.

All around you, screaming orcs leap from the wall, forcing the remaining pockets of resistance to retreat and reform around Fostyr at the opening to the underground tunnels.

You stagger toward your friend. Fostyr sees you and gestures wildly for you to hurry. With a sideways blow, he shatters a spear with his sword, then runs his blade through the chest of the attacking orc.

As soon as you reach him, Fostyr claps you on the arm with his free hand.

"Get moving," he says. He grins wearily. "I was afraid they'd got you."

And the Dragon's Eye, you think.

"What about you?" you say. "I can't just leave you!"

Fostyr takes a deep breath. "I'll hold them off while you and the others get away. Your mission is more important. Don't worry about me. Just go!"

You hesitate, not certain what to do.

If you retreat into the tunnels, go to 8.
If you stay and fight beside Fostyr, turn to 36.

15

"This way," you say, leading your companions down the shiny passage. "I don't like the looks of that acid in the other branch."

"Look how glossy this tunnel is!" Turloc exclaims. The walls, the ceiling, even the floor are a slick, gleaming black that shimmers in the torchlight.

Relf touches the wall with one finger, puts it to his nose, and makes a face. "It stinks," he says.

"It smells like pitch," you say. "The stuff they use to seal boats."

"What is that stuff doing down here?" Renda asks.

Relf tries to wipe the black stuff off his finger onto his pants. "Hey, it won't come off. It's too sticky."

Turloc shakes his head and scowls. "I don't like the looks of this . . ." he mumbles. The floor squishes slightly as he presses his boot down. "Maybe we should go back and follow the other tunnel."

"We're not getting scared, are we?" says the squat, muscular axe wielder behind him. The blade of his axe clanks against the wall as he moves forward, shouldering Turloc aside.

"I'm not scared," Turloc says brusquely. "Just smart . . . something you wouldn't know about."

The squat man glares at him and waves his axe threateningly.

"Oh, stop it, both of you," Renda scolds. "You're acting stupid."

Fortunately there's little room in the cramped tunnel for a fight. Even so, you don't want any trouble between these two. You step between them. "That's enough!" you say threateningly. "We have plenty of enemies as it is. The last thing we need is to fight among ourselves."

The two men eye each other grudgingly.

"Now let's go," you say. "No more nonsense."

With sideways glances at each other, the men obey.

Turloc steps ahead of you, jingling the chains of his flail, followed by the axe wielder. They start cautiously down the tunnel.

You and the others follow close behind. The passageway is slick, but the rock floor is uneven enough to keep you from slipping.

"So far, so good," Turloc says, grinning at you.

After fifty yards, the tunnel widens into a circular cave with a low ceiling.

"That smell is getting worse," Relf says, wrinkling his nose.

You nod, grimacing. The smell seems to coat your teeth, leaving behind a bitter-tasting, sulfurous scum.

"The floor's getting stickier," Renda says, lifting one foot with a noticeable sucking sound.

"It's getting harder to move my feet," Turloc says. "I vote we turn around."

The tunnel floor creaks underfoot, like thin, snapping ice. "What the—?" exclaims the squat axe wielder as the floor of the tunnel begins to bow beneath his feet.

"The floor's collapsing," Renda shouts, backing hurriedly down the tunnel.

"Everyone out!" you yell, pushing Relf after Renda. You and the others turn, moving as quickly as you can back across the sticky rock.

But the floor has already weakened, a thin crust over an oozing morass. A hole opens up beneath the squat axe wielder's feet. Only a few feet ahead of you, he begins to sink up to his knees in black muck.

You and the others quickly come to a stop. More of your comrades begin to sink. The tunnel floor cracks wider next to you, swallowing Relf.

Renda grabs for her twin, but the crack splits again, dropping her into the gunk.

"Grab my hand!" you say. She reaches out one hand, holding on to Relf with the other. Just as your fingers touch, the rock splits under your feet.

Instinctively you leap to the side. Renda's hand

slips free.

You search for a way to reach her and Relf, but they're too far away, sinking into the thick black ooze.

"Corlen," Renda shouts. "Get out while you can!"

The only way out is deeper into the tunnel. You turn just as another crevice opens. The shifting rock knocks you off balance. All around you, the floor is shattering. You hang for a moment, suspended in space, then topple into the tarry goo. It sucks at your legs, pulling you down as if it is alive and hungry.

The sulfurous smell is overpowering. Dizzy, you look around. All of your companions are trapped like flies in black honey.

You hold your head as high as you can, for as long as you can, hoping your feet will touch bottom soon, but there is no bottom. The ooze keeps drawing you down, deeper and deeper.

The sticky muck reaches your waist, then your chest. You touch the Dragon's Eye beneath your tunic. At least Tyrion will never possess it now.

You struggle, growing more and more exhausted as the goo covers your shoulders, your lips, your nose, your eyes, enveloping you in final darkness.

The End

16

"I'm all right," Renda calls from the pit. Her voice sounds far away, mixed with a faint murmur of running water. "I landed in a stream."

You lean closer. Beside you, Relf heaves a huge sigh of relief.

"It's only about ten feet down," Renda shouts. She peers up at you, her face lit by the flicker of the torches circling the pit as your companions hurry forward to help. "But it sure is cold down here!"

Someone lowers a rope, and Renda grabs it. You,

Relf, and Turloc haul her back up.

Renda crawls over the edge. She's soaked. "The water's only waist deep," she says, flashing a grin.

You wet your dry lips. "Did you taste the water? Can we drink it?"

Renda nods. "A big mouthful, whether I wanted to or not. It's fresh."

You smile. Finally things are starting to look up. "We could use something to eat, too, but the water will hold us for a while."

Holding out your torch, you peer down into the hole. The rock sides angle steeply, slick with moss.

You hand your whip to Relf, then turn to the stooped flail wielder. "Turloc," you say, "give Relf your helmet. Relf, tie my whip to the helmet. Good . . . now lower it into the water."

Relf lowers the helmet into the pit, then hauls it up. Water sloshes over the helmet's sides. Everyone crowds forward to drink deeply; Turloc has to lower the makeshift bucket two more times. At last your thirst is quenched and your stomach feels full from the cold water. Rubbing your hands together, you feel awake and energetic for the first time since you entered the winding catacombs.

"I think we must be getting close to the surface," Renda says.

"How big is the river tunnel?" you ask.

"I was able to stand up without hitting my head. There's a current, but it's not too bad."

"Do you think we can get out by following the river?" Relf asks. "It must go underground some-where."

"Let's have a look," you say, standing. Grabbing a torch and the rope, you walk to the edge of the pit.

Renda and the others follow. You tie the rope around your waist. What will happen if the Dragon's Eye gets wet? It seems as hard as glass, but what if it dissolves like a salt crystal?

It doesn't matter, you tell yourself. If you don't get

out of the caves, the Dragon's Eye is lost anyway. And you along with it.

"I should go," Renda volunteers. "I'm soaked already."

You shake your head. "No. If this works, we'll all have to get wet anyway. Lower me down."

Torch in one hand, you grip the rope with the other, easing yourself over the edge of the pit. Your feet slip on the slick moss as you try to rappel down the moss-slick wall.

The burbling water grows louder. Lowering yourself into the flowing cave river, you feel for the bottom of the stream.

The bottom is almost as slick as the mossy walls. You wedge your boot heels between some rocks to steady yourself against the gentle wash of the current. Bracing yourself, you wade upstream, torch held high. The firelight glints off the ceiling above.

Your head just clears the rocky overhangs, where tiny young stalactites poke downward. The passage continues ahead for as far as you can see. The walls have been worn smooth by the running water, glittering white from quartz and calcite deposits laid down over the centuries. The river seems to hold at about the same waist-high depth. You smile, relieved.

After a few more steps, the rope draws taut. You wade back to the shaft.

Renda leans over the edge of the pit. "Well?" she calls down.

"The way seems clear," you say. "Unless we run into a waterfall, we should be okay. Leave the rope tied to that rock, in case we need to turn around and climb back up."

"What if we need it farther on?" someone asks.

You unfasten your whip and hold it up. "We've got this," you say.

"I'm game to try it," Relf says.

You hear a flurry of enthusiastic agreement from your party.

"All right, then. Let's get going," you say.

It takes Renda a few minutes to tie the rope around the outcropping. She lowers herself down first, and the others follow quickly. A few of them slip and splash in the water, much to the delight of the others. One man goes under, bobbing to the surface and clutching his now useless torch. He tosses it away, sputtering, but the mood of your party is so improved now that even he grins at his misfortune.

When everyone is in the stream, you square your shoulders. "Ready?" you ask.

You slosh upstream, holding the torch high. Straining your ears, you listen for the roar of a waterfall, but you hear only the river's steady gurgling and Relf's soft breathing behind you.

You wade onward. The current quickens as the rock walls narrow. The river pushes at you, as if trying to force you back. Then the ceiling begins to lower. Twenty feet ahead, the ceiling slips below the churning water.

"Now what?" someone groans.

"We turn back," someone else says sullenly. "What a waste of time."

"It might widen out again," you say.

"Even if it does," the spearwoman says, "we won't be able to take torches with us."

True.

You hand your torch to Relf. "Wait here," you say. "Let me check this out. If I'm not back in a few minutes, turn around."

Relf nods. Renda gives you a nod of encouragement. You toy with the idea of passing the Dragon's Eye to Relf or Renda, in case you don't make it, but they might not make it either. The fewer people who know you have the eye, the better. Taking a deep breath, you dive under the water.

Eyes open in the darkness, you kick hard with your legs, your arms stroking through the water like a frog. Your head scrapes the top of the tunnel. You open your eyes. Everything is cold and black.

Panic squeezes your chest. Your lungs ache, desperate for air. Your pulse throbs in your ears. The water is so cold. You lift your head and crack it against the tunnel ceiling.

You start to turn around, afraid you don't have enough air to get back, but suddenly your head breaks the surface. The current threatens to tug you under again, but you plant your feet and reach out with your arms. Your fingers grasp solid rock. You cling to the rock, resting your cheek against its algae-slick surface.

You suck in huge breaths, then raise your head, shivering. You can see! It's nighttime, and the moon shines down with a faint white light, but it looks like a blazing sun to your eyes after so long in the dark caverns. You turn your head. A dim circle of light, framed by brambles, shines down on you.

You shake with relief. You touch the Dragon's Eye. It feels solid.

You take several deep breaths, then duck your head under the water. The trip back is easier, since the current pushes you along. Within seconds, you swim into Relf's legs, knocking him off his balance.

You stand up, dripping, pulling him up with you.

"I found an opening to the outside!" you exclaim. You take a gulp of air. "It's only a little ways. We can get out!"

Renda laughs, breaking the tension, and immediately everyone joins in.

"Come on," she says. "Let's get out of here."

You fill your lungs, then dive again. The trip seems shorter now that you know you can make it.

You do a quick head count after everyone surfaces, then splash toward the mouth of the cave. It opens into a dense forest. It's early evening, and the moon is visible through the tops of the trees. The others gather around you, gaping up at the star-studded sky.

"Does anyone know where we are?" you ask. "Anybody recognize this place?"

"I think so," someone says. "But if I'm right, this forest is probably teeming with orcs."

You chuckle grimly. "Is there any place that isn't?"

You take a deep breath. First things first. You can take the Dragon's Eye to Crockport in the morning. For now, you and the others need food and rest.

"First we'll secure the area," you say. "Then let's see what kind of meal we can scrape together from the forest."

Relf hisses behind you. You turn quickly to see Renda bending over her twin brother. Curled on the ground, Relf clutches his ankle, wincing in pain. "I slipped," he says. "I think my ankle is broken."

With a broken ankle, Relf will never be able to outrun an orc. You look around. Nothing disturbs the evening quiet. "You might be safer staying here," you say. "We'll be back for you. We're just going to scout the area and find some food."

He nods.

"I'm staying with him," Renda says decisively. "Don't worry, Corlen. We'll keep ourselves hidden."

"All right." You nod somberly. The Dragon's Eye hangs heavy on your chest. "We'll be back soon."

Go to 10.

17

You point down the tunnel with the small pools of acid. "The other tunnel looks too cramped. We'll be able to move more quickly down this one."

Renda takes out her bow. "Let's keep our eyes open, though."

The acid fumes are so strong you can taste them. The inside of your mouth feels as though it's on fire. Your eyes begin to water. Your throat feels as if it's a raw blister, and your lungs heave painfully. It becomes impossible to speak after going only a short distance.

Everyone is coughing and wiping his eyes. You try to breathe through your nose, but the burning stench assaults your nostrils.

You pull one corner of your cloak up to cover your nose and mouth. Except for your eyes, the burning eases somewhat. Your comrades follow your example. Their coughing diminishes as they trudge forward.

After a hundred yards, the puddles become less numerous and get smaller. The air clears a bit, and you can feel a thin breeze from above. Your eyes continue to water, but the stinging sensation eases. Your lungs begin to clear.

The acid fumes have parched your mouth. Your tongue is cracked and swollen. Among your entire party, only a few sips of water remain.

You study the walls around you. The tunnel is unnaturally glassy and smooth. Maybe miners cut it, using the acid. If so, you might be close to the surface.

You wonder fleetingly if the acid would dissolve the Dragon's Eye. You force the thought aside. Destroying the eye isn't the answer. You need to get the eye to Count Delwyn in Crockport, where it can be used to protect the land rather than destroy it.

You hurry on. A second tunnel angles off to the left, and you check it out. Rougher and less even, this one doesn't seem to have any acid. The air smells fresher. With a sigh of relief, you unwrap the cloak from your face. Motioning to your group, you set off down the new passage.

Finally you seem to be getting somewhere. The tunnel floor slopes steadily upward, past many smaller caves and tunnels. You push on, tired but too excited to stop to rest. Your long underground journey could finally be over.

Relf hurries ahead, the flicker of his torch bobbing in the darkness.

Suddenly the torch stops. "Caves," he shouts back at you. "Lots of them."

You hurry to join him. Standing beside the bronze-haired twin, you turn slowly, gazing at the series of caves around you. The air seems fresh and cool. Hope rises in your chest. "Spread out!" you say. "See if you can find a way out. This fresh air has to be coming from somewhere."

Everyone heads off in different directions.

You enter a tiny chamber, but it's filled with rubble. Backing out, you move on to the next cavern. Although much larger, this one is no more helpful than the first. You enter a third chamber. Little more than a narrow hallway blocked by a giant slab of rock, it doesn't seem to have a ceiling. Curious, you raise your torch.

Hundreds of fluttering black wings swoop down, shrieking at the upper range of human hearing. You thrash out with your arms, protecting your eyes as the bats flap around your head and shoulders. You swing your torch like a club, stunning several bats and knocking them to the ground. Then you turn and run, retracing your steps.

Panting for breath, you watch as the bats vanish into blackness. There must be a way out nearby.

Encouraged, you rush into the next cave. Foul air weighs on you. You gag on the stench of rotting flesh.

Not only does the chamber reek, but its shape reminds you of an eye socket in a human skull. Raising your torch, you look around. Manacles hang from the walls. Torn, bloody clothing and a shield lie on the floor beneath the wrist irons. Fresh bones clutter the ground beneath three unlit torches high on the chamber wall.

The hair on the back of your neck prickles. Fostyr told you that chambers like this riddle these tunnels, each guarded by some unknown monster.

You start to back out, then notice three torches jammed into low crevices. Unlike the others, these are easily within reach. Your party could certainly use them. You creep forward cautiously.

A bone snaps underfoot. Fear spikes through you. You yank the torches from the wall. Another bone snaps, as if cracked by jaws.

Torches in hand, once again you begin to back out cautiously, afraid that whatever feeds on the chained prisoners may be watching you even now. Cold sweat chills the back of your neck.

Someone shouts from one of the other caves. You dash out of the chamber, dropping the newfound torches. Your shoulder blades tense, awaiting some kind of attack.

Nothing happens.

Another shout echoes through the caves.

You run toward the voice, drawing your oaken sword as you go. Light flickers around a big outcropping of stone ahead. Your companions are gathered around Relf.

"What's going on?" you ask, gasping for breath.

A pike carrier steps aside, letting you squeeze in through the circle. Renda kneels beside Relf. She holds his right hand gently, examining it.

Relf looks up at you. "I burned myself exploring a tunnel," he says.

"Will he be all right?" you ask Renda.

She presses her lips together. "I think so," she says. "There are only a few blisters. I wish we had some cold water we could soak his hand in."

"I'll be okay," Relf says, starting to rise.

"Where's the tunnel where it happened?" you ask.

"In the next cave. I'll show you." Hugging his hand to his chest, Relf leads you to the cavern.

The reek of acid hits you before you reach the opening. You hold out your torch and start slowly down the passage, Relf and Renda on either side. The tunnel comes to a dead end after only a few yards. The rock wall in front of you is cracked and soft-looking, like strange, warm clay.

Renda pokes at it with her torch.

The rock shifts suddenly, then rumbles toward you. You back up quickly, fearing another cave-in.

The oozing rock follows you out of the tunnel and

into the cave, like a wad of mobile mud.

"It's alive!" Relf shouts, scampering out of the way.

The thing stops just outside the tunnel opening. It looks like a huge stone slug. It reeks of acid. It rears up, looming large in the dimness.

Renda inhales sharply. "It's a horgar," she says softly. "I've heard people talk about them, but I always figured they were just stories."

"What kind of stories?" you ask.

"Horgars live underground," she says. "They secrete acid to burrow through rock. Miners talk about them."

The horgar scuttles toward Relf, forcing him back against the cave wall, then hesitates. "Help!" Relf shouts, looking frantically toward you and his sister.

You stiffen. The horgar might leave Relf alone if you don't provoke it. But it might also attack him. Renda looks desperately toward you.

Should you attack the creature?

If you elect to attack the horgar, go to 12.
If you choose not to attack the horgar, turn to 6.

18

You follow the ravine into the forest quietly. You need to make your way south, along the shore of the lake, to the city of Crockport, where you can deliver the eye to safety. Coiling your whip in one hand, you set out, ducking low, hoping to remain unseen.

With a yell of alarm, an orc rushes at you from one side, swinging a spiked mace. You crack your whip, snapping the orc's wrist. The creature drops the heavy mace, its angry shriek cut short when you lash out again, this time wrapping the whip around its throat. The orc slumps at your feet, its neck broken.

But the alarm has been raised, and more orcs set

out after you in pursuit.

A shout rises from the trees to your right. The forest is crawling with orcs. You're convinced you'll never make it out alive, but you keep running, dodging trees. Up ahead, the forest clears again, and you see Whyestil Lake.

A memory flashes to your mind. On routine patrol duty, you recall seeing a pier and an abandoned boat not far from here. If you can get to the boat, you'll have a better chance of escaping. Orcs hate water.

Forsaking caution, you race toward the rocky shore of the lake, letting your whip dangle behind you. Three orcs dart from the oak grove off to your left, trying to cut you off.

You flick your whip at the nearest one, an ugly brute with a white scar across its chin like a second mouth. The orc ducks, only to have the whip's recoil loosen its grip on the rusty pike it carries. With a well-aimed kick, you knock the pike from its hand. Your boot crushes the orc's fingers. It howls and bends over, cradling its hand.

The second orc, this one brandishing a sword, swerves, sidestepping its comrade. You back away, flexing and unflexing your wrist, waiting for the right moment to strike with the braided leather whip. You try to keep an eye on the two orcs in front of you while you look for the third. Where did it go? Your shoulder blades twitch at the thought of the third orc's halberd slicing across your back.

Cocking your wrist, you get ready to strike out at the orc with the sword when you hear a twig snap behind you. You whirl, twirling the long whip in a protective arc around your body. The sword-wielding orc screams as its sword clatters to the ground. As you complete the circle, your whip flicks across the chest plate of the third orc. It swipes at your whip and misses.

Snapping at the orcs once more to make them stumble backward, you set out at a run again, leaping over roots and logs. As you clear a tangle of brambles, two thick trees block your path. Bounding between them, you are jerked backward suddenly as the end of your whip catches on a thick vine. A *whoosh* of air fans your scalp as you lose your balance and tumble backward. With a loud *thwack*, the third orc's halberd buries itself in the trunk of a tree just beside your head. Unable to stop, the orc careens past you.

You roll aside as the first orc charges with its pike. You dive through the brambles, clawing your way through their thorny branches. You emerge snagged and scratched, but you don't dare slow down.

You burst from the forest, the orcs in pursuit. You can hear them huffing and snorting close behind you. Your lungs ache as you force yourself to run faster. Your feet kick up shards of gravel on the stony beach.

Someone shouts your name. You look up. The lake is only a few feet away. Just as you expected, the pier stretches in front of you like a drawbridge, blocked by another fierce skirmish raging on the banks of the lake. It's a group of fighters, and in a flash, you recognize the decoy party, the ones Captain Jongh sent out with the false eye.

Grigneth holds the pouch in his hand, trying to protect it, and as you watch, one of the orcs snatches it away. "Eye! Me have eye!" the orc shouts, dancing in triumph.

"Give it back!" Grigneth cries, as if he really expects the orc to listen to him.

The orc tears open the sack to look at the Dragon's Eye, but he removes only a smooth, round stone. "Fake!" the orc howls. "Get them!"

Still mounted on their horses, Beatrix, with her sharp wooden lance, and rotund Vystan fight valiantly against a handful of enraged orcs. Beside them, stubble-bearded Grigneth battles on foot, looking terrified. This is the man, you realize, who was given charge of the decoy eye.

Beatrix spots you. She whacks her opponent across

the head, then gestures with her lance. "Corlen!"

You turn. Two of the others, grim-faced Bresnor, the archer, and Peri, a powerful swordsman with a drooping black mustache, have broken free of the orc attack. They race toward the pier. You sprint after them. Bresnor glances over his shoulder, then stops, turning to face you.

He shouts something you can't hear, then raises his bow and aims directly at you. Before you can duck, an arrow whizzes past your head. You hear a thud behind you, followed by a sharp cry.

You whirl around, lashing the whip in a now-familiar circle. But this time you lift the circle higher, hoping to catch the remaining orc across the eyes or throat.

As the whip slices the orc's cheek, another arrow nicks your ear. Too close! Before you can shout for Bresnor to be careful, his third arrow finds its target. The orc grasps its shoulder and falls to its knees.

You turn and run toward the pier and the waiting boat as two more orcs dash from the forest.

Go to 21.

19

"It'll be dawn in a few hours," Fostyr whispers. "If we're going to get out of here, we'd better do it soon."

You look over to the orcs, who are still laughing and cuffing each other near the firelight. You wonder how long it will be before they get hungry again.

Under a partly cloudy sky, the stars are fading over Whyestil Lake, washed by the approaching dawn. To the west, the moon is setting behind the wall of trees that marks the edge of Vesve Forest.

"I agree . . . especially since they still haven't found the eye," you say under your breath. "Any ideas?"

"That pile of weapons over there." Fostyr gestures

with his chin at the weapons captured by the orcs. "See that sword near the pile?"

You peer at the jumble of spears, axes, and bows lit by the flickering glow of the guards' campfire. You catch sight of the gleaming blade of a long sword lying apart from the other weapons.

"Yeah, I see it," you say softly. "But how do we get to it without them seeing us?"

"If one of us stays here, they might not notice."

You glance at the orcs. One of them throws another slab of bloody meat on the fire. The other two are casting dice and arguing over their game.

"You go," Fostyr says.

"I won't be able to bring it back. I can't touch the metal."

"You don't have to bring it back. Just cut your wrists free. We're going to escape, not fight."

You shake your head, dubious.

"Corlen, you're closer and stronger," Fostyr says. "Besides, the metal studs on my tunic will reflect the light."

True enough. For once, not being able to wear metal is an advantage. "All right." You roll quietly away from Fostyr toward the weapons.

With each roll, sharp rocks on the ground dig into your shoulder blades and hips. You try to make as little noise as possible. Beads of sweat break out on your forehead. Dirt cakes your face, and you spit grains of grit from your mouth. At least the smeared grime will make you less visible in the darkness.

It seems to take forever to reach the weapons pile. You tense, trying to shrink into a smaller target. Surely one of the orcs will look up and see you, but they are drunk and preoccupied with their victory and their plunder.

At last the pile of swords is within reach, and you squirm toward it, backing up and feeling with your hands. The pile itself now helps block you from view.

The sword rests on the ground, its tip toward you.

You twist your neck around, but no matter how hard you try, you can't see the sword. You take a deep breath, clench your teeth, and carefully search for the blade, dreading the touch of the metal.

Magical fire sears the tip of your right index finger. You jerk your finger away, a heat blister forming under the skin.

You reach for the sword again, more carefully this time. After the blade nicks your finger, you dig at the ground next to it, scraping out a shallow hole into which you can slide one hand.

Cautiously you spread your hands as far apart as you can and begin to saw at the leather cords with the edge of the sword, trying not to let the metal touch your exposed skin. The blade nicks you several times, raising welts, but after several tense minutes, you feel the leather thong break. Your hands come free, and you hold them in front of you with a gasp of relief. Returning circulation makes your hands throb.

Excitement dampens the pain of the metal burns. You quickly untie your ankles and glance at the orc guards, who are still arguing over their game of dice.

You are about to crawl back when you notice your whip and oaken sword lying beside the pile. There's no mistaking them. You glance up at the squabbling guards once more, then quietly retrieve your weapons from the pile before crawling back to Fostyr.

"Well done," he whispers as you untie his hands and feet. "Ah, that feels good," he says with a sigh as the bonds come loose.

"Relax later. Let's go," you say, despite your uncertainty about how both of you are going to slip out of camp without being seen.

"Wait . . . I need a sword for myself," Fostyr says. "We're probably going to have to fight our way out." He crawls on his elbows and knees toward the pile.

You follow him, slowed by your own weapons. Fostyr reaches out and begins hunting for a sword among the booty.

You hear an animal-like shout behind you. The sound jolts through your body. You leap to your feet, ready to do battle again. The guards snatch up their weapons, forgetting their dice but swaying from too much drink. Fostyr drags two long daggers from the pile and quickly hurls them at the orcs. One of the orcs stumbles and falls, a knife buried in its chest. Fostyr yanks a long sword and a small axe from the pile, and the other weapons fall with a clatter. Forgetting stealth, you both run toward the forest.

The remaining two guards sprint after you. One of them trips over the fallen orc's body and sprawls to the ground. Several orcs come running from other campfires. In a moment, dozens of the monster soldiers will be after you.

"Split up!" Fostyr yells. "It'll be hard to follow both of us." He tosses the axe at one of the oncoming orcs. The orc dodges to one side, but the axe catches it in the arm. The orc curses and drops its halberd.

You hesitate, reluctant to leave your friend.

"Go!" Fostyr says. "Save the eye! I'll be okay."

The entire camp seems to have been aroused. Confused shouts fill the air from all sides.

Much as you hate to admit it, you know Fostyr is right. The Dragon's Eye talisman is your first priority. "I'll meet you in Crockport," you say.

Fostyr grins. "Buy me a tankard of ale . . . a big one!"

You turn and sprint for the dim trees at the edge of camp. Sword in hand, you dodge past the forms of the groggy, hung-over orcs as they sit up and peer around them, confused by all the commotion.

An orc blunders into your path, and you smack at its face with the flat of your wooden sword, knocking the creature to the ground.

You glance back. Foystr has stopped by one of the piles of weapons. In a frenzy of fighting, he impales an orc with a spear, then drags out another spear and hurls it at a pack of orcs.

You stagger to a stop at the edge of the camp as a group of orcs races toward you. You see no way to get past them to Fostyr, no way to save him.

Fostyr lied to you. You see now that he had no intention of escaping but merely intended to buy time for you to get away with the Dragon's Eye.

You touch the bulge above your belt where the eye rests against your ribs. You know you'd have done the same for him if the roles were reversed. Still, a knot of shame tightens your throat. Ignoring it, you turn and run, putting on a burst of speed as you see the refuge of the forest straight ahead.

You glance over your shoulder. The orcs are closing the gap, waving their weapons and wasting energy with yells and curses.

A lichen-crusted boulder looms in your path. You dart to the right of it and trip on a smaller rock, falling to one knee. Somehow you regain your feet without missing a step. An arrow whistles over your head. The forest is growing denser, but it gets much thicker just a short sprint away. If you can get that far, you might be able to elude the pursuers. Your lungs feel as if they're about to explode. The shouting of orcs spurs you on.

Suddenly you stumble into a shallow gully cut by flash floods. You roll down the side, bruising your left hip and knee. When you regain your balance, you find you are standing in the dark opening of a cave under a rocky overhang.

Hiding in the concealing bushes, taking a moment to catch your breath, you quickly retie the thong of the Dragon's Eye pouch around your neck so that the pouch hangs against your chest once again.

If you follow the ravine, the forest appears to get much thicker, and you could hide from the orcs. On the other hand, you might be able to disappear into the cave without a trace . . . or you might also get trapped there. You hear the orcs crashing closer, searching for you.

If you decide to enter the cave, turn to 4.
If you elect to follow the ravine into the forest, turn to 18.

20

You and Alix slip down the stairs to the small courtyard at the base of the tower. Clouds roll in from the lake, smearing the night sky and blotting out the moon. Around the tower, you hear many other fighters moving cautiously. Everyone seems tense.

Two fighters jostle past you on their way up the stairs. "Where do you two think you're going?" one of them says, pushing her torch close to you so that the light glares in your face.

"Uh . . . to the privy," you say, covering your eyes from the bright light.

"Me, too," Alix says. "And if you don't let us pass, don't blame us for the mess."

One of the fighters, a female archer, mumbles something, then turns away and hurries up the stairs. Her sturdy boots click on the stone stairs as she goes about her business. The other fighter follows her.

Torches smolder in metal sconces mounted on the courtyard walls, illuminating the meager stockpile of supplies that have been gathered for the siege. Barrels of water, to quench fires set by the orcs as much as to slake the thirst of the soldiers, are stacked beside the stable. Inside the rickety shelter hang sacks of potatoes and strips of salted meat. In the forge next door, the blacksmith's hammer clangs loudly by torchlight, pounding out crossbow bolts as fast as he can. The acrid stench of charcoal hangs in the air, accompanied by the sizzle of quenched metal.

The north gate is closed, barred on the inside. The south gate stands ajar, but it's heavily guarded. Captain Jongh paces nearby, talking to a messenger. He turns every few steps to shout last-minute instructions. You suspect that he must have sent some of his best scouts to spy on the orc encampment.

"We'll have to go over the wall," Alix whispers.

You nod, then move quickly to the sturdy water barrels stacked in a rounded pyramid beside the stable. You look around for Fostyr, but you can't find him in all the confusion. He might have gone over the wall already, probably not wanting to admit to you that he, too, was eager to escape. You shake your head. So much for friendship.

A pang of guilt stings your stomach. There's a chance that Fostyr might still be within the walls, even on his way back to the battlements. What will he do when he finds you missing? Why didn't he tell you where he was going? With Fostyr at your side, you would have had a better chance. You have no particular love for big, straw-haired Alix, but he's a better companion than none.

"Well, are we going or aren't we?" Alix whispers.

"We're going," you say firmly. You decide to forget about Fostyr. If you don't look out for yourself, no one else will. It's time to make your own decisions instead of letting other people make them for you. You're tired of sitting back and following orders while others cause trouble. You remember how helpless you felt when Tyrion killed your father and laughed at you when he placed his curse on you. In the shadows of the tower perimeter walls, with the bloodthirsty orc army camped nearby preparing to attack, you decide that you will never again sit back and wait.

You slip behind the barrels, hidden now from the turmoil in the courtyard and the soldiers on the roof of the stable. You climb to the top of the barrels, carefully avoiding the iron bands holding the slats together. The barrels are full, and your feet and knees make muffled, liquid-sounding reverberations as you work your way higher on the stack. One barrel, resting loosely atop the others, wobbles as you step on it, but you quickly place your hands against the high wall to regain your balance. A flash of cold sweat beads on your skin, and after a moment's pause, you continue to climb.

Below, Alix follows, watching your efforts. From the top of the stack of barrels, you scan the courtyard one last time. You feel mixed emotions at leaving this ramshackle tower in the wilderness. It hasn't been a pleasant assignment, but you are reluctant to leave everyone else to what seems certain doom.

"Come on!" Alix whispers. "Don't just sit there. Someone will spot you!"

You duck your head, but no one is watching. You pull yourself onto the rim of the earthen wall. Broken stones gouge your stomach. You swing your legs over. Pebbles trickle down the sides, pattering on the leaf-strewn ground twenty feet below. Finding a toehold, you lower yourself carefully, scraping the stones, until you hang by your hands.

With a grunt, Alix climbs to the top of the wall and looks down.

Trying not to think of the long drop, you let go, falling to the ground. You slide against the rough, piled earth wall to slow your descent, but still your feet sting when you hit the ground. Alix thuds beside you, letting out a loud *whoof* of air.

"Over there!" whispers a guard on the stable roof, just on the other side of the wall. "Call the archers."

You freeze. Alix drags you into the shadows beneath the wall, pressing your back against the hard-packed dirt.

"Where?" another guard says in a low voice.

"There," says the first.

You imagine him pointing directly at you, but you're too frightened to look up. You're certain they'll spot your pale face in the diffuse moonlight. Your pulse races.

"I don't see anything," the second guard says.

"Well, I'm sure I heard something," says the first. "Toss a torch down there."

Alix taps you on the arm urgently and nods in the direction of the lake and the thick forest. He's right. If you wait any longer, you're sure to be discovered. You'd probably be killed for deserting.

"Better notify Cap'n Jongh," the second guard says.

You run with your head bent down, zigzagging to avoid being hit by an arrow if the guards start shooting. You try to be quiet, but your panicked flight makes crashing sounds in the underbrush.

"There they go!" the first guard shouts.

A crossbow bolt whizzes by within inches of your head. Panting, you put on a burst of speed. Alix shouts something but keeps running.

Your foot catches on a rock, and you slam to the ground. You roll once, wincing as your wooden sword digs into your hip, then you scramble to your feet, running as fast as you can, snapping twigs and crashing through leaves. Your lungs ache.

You should be out of sight by now, especially with the moon behind the clouds. You can still hear a commotion on the tower walls, but the forest has swallowed you up. It's time now to be quiet, to escape silently into the forest.

After all, you still have the Dragon's Eye. Captain Jongh was right to trust you. By yourself, you can slip past all the guards and take it south to your home city of Crockport.

Alix pants heavily a few yards off to your right. He stops to catch his breath. You slow down.

"We made it," he gasps between breaths.

"Yeah," you say. "For a second there, I didn't think we would."

Behind you, the tower is a dark inkblot against the sky. Off to your left, the orc campfires burn brightly.

"Let's head south," you say. "There'll be fewer orcs in that direction. They're going to be interested in the tower, not in a few deserters."

"Too late," Alix says.

You look to where he's pointing. Yellow eyes gleam

between the trees. As your eyes grow more accustomed to the murky light, you see a large party of orcs encircling you. Chuckling wickedly to themselves, they step out from the shadows, drawing their sharp, clumsy weapons. You realize you are hopelessly outnumbered.

You smile weakly, then pull out your white handkerchief. Tying it to the top of your bow, you wave it at the orcs.

"Hey, wait! We've come to join you," Alix says. "Just like your messenger offered."

"Put weapons down," one of the orcs grunts. You drop your bow to the ground, then slip off your quiver, braided leather whip, and oaken sword. Though your weapons aren't particularly deadly, you feel helpless without them. Alix tosses his axe aside and holds his hands up.

"We surrender," Alix says, smiling nervously. You can see the sweat soaking his blond hair. "Under the terms you shouted up to us."

The largest creature strides forward. It's an orog, larger and more cunning than any orc. Taller than the others, it has purplish skin and carries a massive club that resembles an uprooted tree stump with wicked-looking iron hooks protruding from the sides. Four orcs creep closer, hovering at the orog's side. They brandish poleaxes, halberds, and spears, jabbing the air in front of them with threatening motions.

"Me Gorak," the orog rasps. Its breath stinks of putrid meat, as if a small animal has crawled down its throat and died. You almost gag on the stench, turning your face away.

Gorak notices the lump under your jerkin and jabs a gnarled, squarish finger at you, poking your chest. "What under shirt?" Gorak asks insistently, then reaches for the pouch around your neck. You flinch backward, but the point of an orc spear stops you. Your skin sizzles where the metal tip presses between your shoulder blades.

With a grunt of impatience, Gorak tears the pouch from your neck, then opens the pouch and begins to laugh, holding up the petrified Dragon's Eye.

Alix's jaw drops open, and he looks at you in astonishment. "Where did you get that?"

The orog leers at you, its pointed teeth slick with drool. "Tyrion be very happy to have Dragon's Eye."

Too late, you notice the raven's head amulet around Gorak's neck. It's the symbol of the wizard Tyrion, the same sorcerer who killed your father and placed the curse on you. Your blood runs cold.

"We have midnight snack," says one of the orcs behind you, poking again with his spear, deeper this time. "Tender enough."

"We don't want to die," you say, trying to think fast, but despair fills you. "We're here to take you up on your offer. To join you."

The orog sneers, and the rest of the orcs chuckle, as if you've just told them a joke.

"Deserters," Gorak says. "We not want cowards."

The orog nods, staring at the treasured eye. Laughing, the orc closest to Alix swings its halberd. Before your companion can shout or try to run, his head tumbles to the ground.

A moment later sharp, blistering pain stabs through your back and out your chest. You smell burning flesh. The last thing you see is the iron tip of a spear in front of you, your blood boiling on the cold metal point.

The orcs keep laughing in the background, until, for you, it is . . .

The End

21

The boat isn't far, just at the end of the rickety pier, but the orcs won't make it easy for you. You'll have to battle every step of the way, but if you can only make it to the water, push off in the flimsy boat, and pull out into the choppy waters where the orcs can't reach you or your companions, you'll be safe.

Cold air whistles in your throat as you sprint toward the pier. Water slaps the sides of the narrow pier as you race along it toward the boat. Your feet pound against the splintering, rotted wood.

Bresnor and Peri are already on board, hacking at the thick ropes binding the boat to the pier. Running for the small vessel, Grigneth, Beatrix, and Vystan are close behind you as the orcs scream in outrage.

Glancing over your shoulder, you see Beatrix half-dragging Grigneth, his arm flung over her shoulder. His leg is bleeding. "Come on! Hurry!" you shout.

From the boat, Bresnor reaches out to you just as Peri finishes sawing through the thick rope with his bloodied sword blade. Peri tosses the ropes into the boat while portly Vystan helps Beatrix get Grigneth aboard. "Corlen! Look out!" Bresnor shouts.

Instinctively you duck sideways as an arrow buries itself in the soft planking next to you. An orc stands halfway down the pier, already nocking its bow for a second shot. Behind it, another orc shoves the archer out of the way, toppling the creature into the water as the larger orc charges at you with axe raised.

"I'll hold them off!" Peri shouts, stepping out of the boat onto the rickety pier. Gripping the hilt of his weapon with two calloused hands, he raises his notched sword to meet the attack.

Taking no time to argue, you leap into the boat, expecting it to sink at any moment. The clash of metal on metal rings out as Peri slams his sword blade into the descending edge of the orc's battle-axe. Its arms ringing from the impact, the orc tumbles into the lake. At the base of the pier, another orc leaps from the gravel beach to take its place, bounding across the damp planks. Peri grunts, taking a step backward. Fortunately for him, the orcs can only attack one at a

time on the narrow pier. Peri grins through his drooping black mustache and dispatches the second orc,
who falls into the water beside its companion.

Bresnor nocks an arrow. You and Beatrix grab the
oars.

"Come on!" you shout to Peri as a third orc comes
up to challenge him.

Peri nods. With a fierce thrust, he dispatches his
opponent, then turns and leaps for the boat. The
dying orc slumps onto the pier, blocking several orcs
behind it as it clutches the open wound in its chest.
Peri scrambles into the boat.

"Go!" you shout to Beatrix. She matches your
stroke as you dig your oar into the water, pulling hard.
The boat shoots away from the dock. Vystan bails out
the water in the bottom of the boat. You just hope the
rickety craft holds together under the strain.

Clumsy footsteps rattle on the pier. Two orcs, cursing and shouting, run to the end. One of them, bow
already drawn, nocks an arrow and lets it fly. It grazes
Peri's chain mail with a burst of sparks. Skimming the
waves, the arrow disappears into the lake's depths.

Bresnor stands up in the wobbly boat, holds his
longbow in front of him, and takes aim at the orcs. A
smile of anticipation flickers across his normally dour
face. Bresnor shoots, and his black arrow plants itself
firmly in the chest of the nearest orc. The bowman
nocks a second arrow, but the rocking of the boat
sends his shot astray.

You and Beatrix continue to row, wheezing with the
effort, concentrating only on your escape. You can't
allow yourself even to think of Fostyr, or what the orcs
might be doing with him now.

A jagged spear, thrown from the beach by the great
orog commander, pierces the side of the small craft,
just below Beatrix's oarlock.

"That was too close for comfort," the blonde warrior says, rowing harder.

"Get us out of here!" Grigneth cries.

Bresnor scowls. Defiant, he nocks a third arrow and takes careful aim. "Just like shooting from a horse," he mutters, loosing the arrow.

A shriek erupts from the group of orcs clustered at the end of the pier, and there is a loud splash as one of the orcs collapses into the lake. The footsteps of the others make a thunderous sound as the rest of the orcs flee from the splintering pier.

Waves pound the hull of your boat as it slices through the water. Soon you will be out of range.

"Pull harder!" you shout to Beatrix. "Pull!"

"You just concentrate on keeping up with me!" she shouts back.

Just when you think you have escaped, an arrow whispers out of the darkness. Peri grunts and doubles over, clutching at the shaft sticking out of his stomach. Grigneth shies away from the injured man, his eyes white with terror, his mouth open wide.

Bresnor stands up in the rocking stern of the boat and, snarling for revenge, he fires another arrow. But the boat is too far from the pier. The arrow splashes harmlessly into the lake.

"Head south," you tell Beatrix, pulling hard on your oar. The boat angles southward. You breathe easier. The rowing settles into a steady rhythm, and the night folds over the boat.

In the bottom of the small craft, Bresnor and Vystan try to make Peri comfortable. Vystan gets out his dagger and slits Peri's shirt to get at the arrow. "Buck up, Peri," Vystan says with forced cheerfulness. "It's only a flesh wound."

Peri winces and turns away. The arrow has dug deep. Bresnor glares at Vystan. "You think life is just one big joke, don't you?" he says in a low, cold voice.

Behind you, Grigneth laughs bitterly, holding his hand over his bloody leg. "That's what he said to me, too," Grigneth says. "Only a flesh wound. Hah! I'm dying."

"Only if you don't shut up," Bresnor says.

Grigneth winces, probing his wounded thigh with his fingers, preoccupied with his minor injury. Letting go of the oar with one hand, you touch the pouch beneath your jerkin. The Dragon's Eye is safe. You are thankful the precious talisman is in your possession. You grab the oar again and concentrate on matching Beatrix's rhythm. You should be long gone by morning. You will have left Fostyr far behind, beyond any hope of rescue. You swallow hard.

The steady rhythm of the rowing calms you a little—everything but your mind. You keep seeing Fostyr, alone, surrounded by orcs and fighting to defend you. You grind your teeth. The orcs will pay for this. And if you ever confront him face to face, the wizard will pay an even higher price.

In the bottom of the boat, Peri bites back a scream of pain. "Got it out," Vystan grunts.

You look up. Bresnor holds the bloodied arrow Vystan has removed from Peri. Even by the cloud-shrouded moonlight, Peri's face is pale. He's lost a lot of blood. You wonder if he's going to survive until you reach Crockport. Setting his longbow aside, Bresnor crawls between you and Beatrix to talk to Peri. Vystan bathes the swordsman's wound with lake water, then rolls up his own sleeve and cleans a gash across his forearm.

Another flesh wound, you think, suddenly grateful for Vystan's attempts to soothe Peri with humor. You keep rowing.

"What about me?" Grigneth demands.

"You'll be all right," Bresnor shoots back.

After a while, colors filter in with the predawn light. You tell stories to each other to pass the time. You slow your pace to give your shoulders some much-needed rest. Behind you, Grigneth and portly Vystan doze off, snoring loudly. In front of you, Bresnor lolls against the side of the boat, his mouth slack in a sleep of deep exhaustion. Peri wheezes. Is he just resting, you wonder, or is he dying?

You peer into the gray light. Dark blood pools in the bottom of the boat around Peri, still oozing from his wounds. You shudder. The swordsman is probably dying after all.

Beatrix rolls her shoulders and stretches, blinking her bright eyes. You massage your own aching shoulders as she turns in her seat to face Grigneth and Bresnor. She kicks their feet, waking them. "Hey!" she says. "How about taking over for a while?"

Grigneth opens one eye. "I can't," he says. "I'm wounded."

"Would you like to be wounded even worse?" she answers him in a threatening voice.

Grudgingly Grigneth pushes you aside and takes your oar. His color has returned.

Beatrix kicks Bresnor's shin. "Get up, you lazy dragon spawn! Now!"

Bresnor snorts and shakes himself. He changes places with Beatrix, gripping her oar.

Exhausted, you and Beatrix lean against each other. Beatrix falls asleep instantly. You watch the first rays of sun touch the rippling waters of the lake as you continue your journey.

Go to 5.

22

You decide the cave is your best chance for now. You turn and sprint for the jagged opening, taking the orcs who had been waiting for you by surprise. Ducking your head, you plunge through the dangling willow fronds, diving from the moonlit evening into blackness. The two orcs scramble after you, weapons and armor clanking loudly. Even with all that added weight, they seem to be gaining on you. You know you would never have made it past them to the pier.

Leathery wings brush your face as a cloud of bats

pours out of the dark tunnel. You slip on the muddy
cave floor, sprawling face first in the muck. Slime
coats your chest and oozes down the neck of your
leather armor. Shadows block the feeble light from the
cave opening—it's the orcs, standing just outside the
cave mouth, peering inside.

You scramble to your feet, grasping at a tree root
poking out of the crumbling cave wall beside you. You
glance over your shoulder at the opening to the lakeshore, where your companions continue the battle.
The two orcs grunt, pointing in your direction.

Gasping for breath, you stumble deeper into the
dark cave, guiding yourself along the walls. Water
beads along the rock like perspiration. Another flurry
of bats sweeps past you, stirring the still air. The
stench of mold fills your lungs. You force yourself not
to cough and give your position away.

The passage slopes down into the earth. You creep
along the rough wall, each step taking you deeper into
the cold, damp, dark cave. You hear two sets of heavy
orc footsteps sloshing through the muck behind you.
You flatten yourself into a gap in the wall. You hear a
thud, then a loud grunt. You smirk. One orc has hit its
head on a low ceiling and fallen. You imagine the
other stopping and helping the first orc to its feet,
cuffing its companion for being so clumsy.

You stand still in the darkness, waiting for the orcs
to pass. Before long, they tramp past you, one of them
brushing your muddy chest as it goes by. You turn to
flee from the cave. Perhaps now the battle has waned
and you can make it to the boat. Or perhaps your
companions have all been killed, and you will have to
continue the mission alone.

But when you approach the entrance, you see the
silhouette of an orog guarding the mouth of the cave.
You finger the handle of your whip, but there is no
room to lash out with it in the narrow tunnel. Just
beyond the orog, you see more orcs swarming about.
You clench your teeth in frustration and pad silently

after the first two orcs. Maybe there's another way out. The tunnels seem to be a maze.

You hear the two orcs whispering somewhere off to the left. You come to a place where the tunnel forks. You take the fork to the right, away from the creatures. A surge of hope drums in your chest. Perhaps the gods are with you after all. You have the Dragon's Eye, and you are safe, temporarily at least.

You creep down the right branch, running a hand along each wall. Pebbles loosen and tumble beneath your fingers. You turn sideways to squeeze between two piles of fallen rock and debris, ducking as the tunnel narrows. You grab an embedded stone and pull yourself through. It rips loose in your hand and clatters to the floor. The cave roof above you shudders as if about to collapse. You hold your breath, afraid you'll be crushed under a ton of loose rock.

Shouts echo from the other branch. The two orcs retrace their steps and splash toward you, shouting something to the burly orog at the mouth of the cave. You hear reinforcements entering into the tunnel.

You scrape quickly by the second rockslide, ignoring the sharp points of rock that gouge your arms. The tunnel widens considerably once you pass the slides. You draw your oaken sword.

You turn to face the narrow opening you have just squeezed through. You dig the tip of the sword into a crack in the protruding rocks and lean into the blade, using the hard oak like a lever. You feel the wall crumble and slip. You leap back just as a small avalanche buries the opening. Moments later, after the clattering of rocks ceases, you hear the muffled curses of the orcs on the other side of the cave-in.

Though it seemed dark before, now there is no light whatsoever. You pat your chest, feeling for the pouch. At least the talisman is still safe. You pull out the leather thong and make sure it is tied firmly around your neck.

Inching forward, you guide yourself along the walls.

You go as fast as you can, not knowing how soon the orcs will dig their way past the rockslide. Your hand glides over algae, rock, and oozing mud. You begin to understand how a blind man must feel.

Hopelessness envelopes you, and you come to a stop. Soft sniffling, squeaking noises echo through the tunnel: rats. A chill crawls up your spine. You hurry on deeper into the tunnel, trying to put some distance between you and the rats and the orcs—and whatever other dangers the cave might have in store for you.

Turn to 4.

23

"I'll stay here at the tower," you say, sounding braver than you actually feel as you envision the over-whelming forces of the orc army. "I think you need me here."

"I'll stay, too," Fostyr says, grinning broadly. "We'll make those orcs think twice."

You smile back, glad you'll be fighting together. You and Fostyr have been through so many cam-paigns together, it's hard to imagine him not guarding your back or you not guarding his. The fighters at Dragon's Eye Tower are a good, dependable crew, and you can't imagine leaving them in their time of great-est danger.

Captain Jongh nods, and when he smiles at you, his jagged, broken nose makes him look like a ferocious animal. "Reinforcements are coming from Crock-port," he says, "but I'm sure they won't arrive in time. We're on our own here."

He narrows his eyes, and a secret glints in his pupils as he bends closer. With a glance from side to side, he lowers his voice. "I'm glad you're staying behind, Corlen. You're the most dependable fighter we have, despite . . ." He glances meaningfully at your wooden sword and your whip, and you know he is thinking of the curse. "Uh, despite your handicap. That's why I have to give you another mission." Captain Jongh swallows, then takes a deep breath, as if it's difficult for him to divulge his secret. You and Fostyr watch him intently, intrigued.

"The escort is a decoy," Captain Jongh whispers. You gasp in disbelief, but the captain holds up his hand and glares at you. "Quiet! Let me explain. We've already flushed out two spies from Iuz, and there are probably more. I doubt the group supposedly escorting the eye will actually make it to Crockport. I've kept the Dragon's Eye here. Once the orcs discover the ruse, they'll think I have the talisman."

He takes a thong with a leather pouch from around his neck, holds it reluctantly for a moment, and finally slips it over your head. Fostyr's eyes go wide with astonishment. "If the decoy doesn't work, and if the orc army breaks through our defenses, they'll be looking for me, not you. Protect the Dragon's Eye at all costs. If it looks like we're going to be overrun, head into the tunnels under the tower. Don't worry about the rest of us. Your primary mission is to keep the real eye safe."

You nod, your mouth dry. You straighten your shoulders and say evenly, "I'll guard it with my life."

"*We* will," Fostyr says, by your side as always.

"I thought so," Captain Jongh says. "Remember, if the tower falls, deliver the eye to Count Delwyn."

"Near Crockport," you say. "I know where his castle is." You tuck the worn leather pouch underneath your jerkin.

Captain Jongh smiles grimly. "Be careful, Corlen. Now I must must see to preparations for battle." He clasps your shoulder, then turns and stalks away.

You glance at the other grim-faced soldiers preparing to defend Dragon's Eye Tower, and then you look out past the battlements to see the roiling chaos of the invading orc army. There don't seem to be enough fighters to hold the decaying old fortress against the force massing on the plain near the shore of Lake Whyestil. A sea of orc campfires stretches far into the distance, flickering like water at sunset. You can almost feel the heat roaring up, ready to consume you. Fear seems to seep deep into your bones. Paying closer attention, you can see the tension in the faces of the other defenders. You know the odds are very much against you.

Instead of warming you, the glow of the orcish encampments sends a sharp chill through your bones. It is not full darkness yet, but you know the army of Iuz will attack before long. The orcs have better night vision than humans and prefer the cover of darkness to strengthen their thirst for battle.

Everyone around you checks and rechecks equipment, tightening bowstrings, fastening armor, stacking piles of arrows within reach, sharpening weapons, filling water buckets in case of an attack by fire. A bucket brigade of soldiers passes skin bags filled with oil from the tower's larders, dumping them into large black caldrons by the perimeter wall. Others pile wood high, lighting blazing fires beneath the kettles. Defenders take position atop the earthen wall, ready to spill the boiling oil down upon the first wave of the orc attack.

Standing on the high wall, you tighten your own leather armor, making sure it's fastened securely, and Fostyr checks the lacings on the back. You help him as best you can, without touching any of his metal chain mail. Together the two of you test your bowstrings. You loosen your whip, letting it hang coiled at your waist within easy reach, opposite your wooden sword. You count forty-three arrows in your quiver—enough to make the orc army pay dearly when they reach the tower. The more orcs you can pick off from a distance, the fewer you'll have to fight at close quarters.

Seven orc scouts venture close to the earthen perimeter walls below the tower, just out of arrow range.

One of them shouts in a loud, guttural language, taunting you. Fostyr taunts the orcs right back. The others spread out, keeping low to the ground, sniffing the dirt and coming as close as they dare. They carry smoking torches to light their way.

"Probably scouting the terrain," Fostyr says.

You nod. "And trying to figure out the best approach for a massed attack. My guess is there are others hiding in the shadows, doing the real scouting. That bunch is too obvious."

In the early dusk, you can just make out the mucous-green skin, ugly snouts, and reddish eyes so typical of orcs. Coarse hair mats their shoulders and arms. They wear splotched leather armor—you've heard rumors that it's made of human skin—studded with metal rivets. Three of the scouts carry huge battle-axes. The remaining four have long swords that gleam in the torchlight. All of them lope along with a swaying, animal-like gait.

Fostyr exhales with a hiss. "Ready?" he asks.

"As ready as I'll ever be," you say, the Dragon's Eye heavy around your neck. You glance uncertainly at the orc patrol. It has moved closer, as if daring you and your companions to attack.

"Hey, Corlen," one of the other guards calls, "how do you expect to kill any orcs with that toy sword? Why don't you fight with a real weapon?"

"Watch what you're saying," Fostyr snaps.

Your blood warms to the challenge. You yank a flint-tipped arrow from your quiver and quickly nock it against the bowstring.

"A real weapon like this?" you call back. You take aim at the nearest orc, a big axe-wielder with stooped shoulders. You grit your teeth, forcing your arms to relax as you draw the bowstring taut.

In happier days, your father taught you to shoot by becoming one with the arrow, seeing your target with your mind as much as your eyes, then releasing the arrow the way a raindrop slides off the end of a leaf—effortlessly and with no wasted motion. Unable to touch metal weapons, you have had nothing to do but practice in the following years.

The arrow hisses through the air toward the over-confident orc scout. Seconds later, a shrill cry pierces the air accompanied by a sound like chopping wood as the arrow strikes home. The orc collapses to the ground, a long feathered shaft protruding from its neck like the stinger of a giant wasp.

Your comrades on the battlements cheer boister-ously. The remaining orcs stare at you in surprise. They leap away, jabbering loudly, and flee back to the safety of their ranks, leaving their dead companion behind in the dust. As they run, one of the orcs howls and raises its sword over its head, swinging it wildly.

The soldier who taunted you whistles in apprecia-tion and taps his metal helmet in a brief salute. One orc more or less won't matter much when they attack, but you have managed to raise the morale of the nearby defenders. Jeering at the retreating orcs, several other archers launch arrows, but the orcs are already too far away.

Fostyr laughs. "*Touché*," he says. "One down. Maybe now they'll think twice before attacking us."

"I doubt it," you say, suddenly having second thoughts. You hope you haven't given the orcs even more incentive to attack. Still, it feels good to prove that you are not helpless, despite the curse you bear.

"Don't worry," Fostyr whispers. "With an aim like that, the eye is in good hands."

You nod, bolstered by his words. Gradually the two of you settle back into your watch, wondering when the orcs will attack. Waiting is the worst part, you think. It would be better to get the attack over with. The night grows cold, and you sidle closer to one of the blazing fires on the battlements. Fostyr gives you some dried meat from his pouch, and you wash it down with water from one of the skins resting against the wall.

Later that night another orc patrol approaches the ramparts. They carry no torches this time, creeping forward like stains in the shadows. It's difficult to make them out in the dim light of the quarter moon that peeks through the clouds.

"What are they doing?" you ask as you and Fostyr peer out at the shadows creeping forward. There aren't enough of them to signal an attack. Still, your heart pounds wildly, and your throat squeezes tight.

"I don't know," Fostyr says.

As you watch, the orcs stop moving forward. They spread out around the earthen perimeter walls, forming a loose circle.

"Fools," one of them shouts, his voice eerie and threatening as it rises out of the darkness. "Humans not win. *Can't* win. Give in now. We not kill you."

"Better live," another one calls. "Be friends."

"Join us," a third one shouts, a new voice from a different part of the circle. "Much money, drink.

Pretty orc females."

"Think, fools," the first orc calls. "Last chance."

"Not think too long," a fourth orc chimes in. "You die thinking."

"One hour," the second orc shouts. "Then no more chance."

A moment later, the orcs leave, melting into the darkness. The sprawling encampment of the huge enemy army appears even more threatening, like a forest fire. You wonder how many more orc reinforcements have appeared under the cover of darkness, or if the orcs have just lit extra campfires to make their numbers appear to have swelled.

The members of the watch around you begin to whisper to each other. Fostyr bites his lower lip thoughtfully. "Stay here," he says. "I want to check on something." Silently he heads down the stairway to the courtyard.

To your left, someone hisses, "It's true. We're all going to die if we stay here."

"Not if we kill them first," a second man says.

The first man laughs a bitter laugh. "Just look at the size of their force! If you think we're going to come out of this alive, you're crazy." He stands and follows Fostyr down the stairs, slinking into the night. Your chest grows cold as you wonder if Fostyr has deserted you after all. Somehow you can't believe he would go away without you—and then you begin to wonder if perhaps you should slip off, too.

Another fighter gets up and quietly slinks away, staying well out of the firelight. Another follows.

A stocky man with yellow hair approaches from behind you. You remember his name is Alix; you met him your first day at Dragon's Eye Tower.

"What do you think, Corlen?" he asks. "I say we try to sneak past those orcs. The eye is already gone, so what's the point in staying here? We'd be throwing our lives away for nothing. If we get caught, we'll just pretend we got sent on a scouting patrol. I say we take our chances!"

You touch your jerkin, the Dragon's Eye pouch a warm bulge next to your skin. It might be better to leave now rather than take the risk of the eye being captured in battle.

It's a gamble either way.

If you decide to leave the tower with Alix, turn to 20.

If you decide to remain in the tower, go to 34.

24

You walk up to the first count. He is more like the Count Delwyn you remember: hands clasped firmly on his sword hilt, protecting his weapon, trusting no one. Suspicion lines his face, but it is out of habit, not malice. You smile, relieved.

"Count Delwyn, I give you the Dragon's Eye," you say. Kneeling, you reach into the mouth of the pouch and lift out the crystalized eye. It gazes coldly at you, its glassy weight dead and brittle in your hand. A chill runs up your spine.

The count studies you, then releases the hilt of his sword and lowers both hands, palms cupped, to receive the talisman.

The second count cries out, knocking Fostyr aside and rushing toward you, sword raised. Throwing all his weight behind the move, burly Vystan wrestles the imposter to the ground and grabs him by both arms. The false count continues to struggle.

"You're making a big mistake," the second count whines. "If you give the eye to your father's murderer, all is lost."

The second count seems too desperate. There is something else as well, simmering beneath his carefully controlled words. It's barely repressed anger— the kind of hidden rage you would expect to see in an evil man like Tyrion.

You let out your breath, raise the eye, and place it and its pouch in the second count's hands.

"Wisely chosen, Corlen," he says, tucking the eye back in its pouch, then slipping the pouch around his neck. "I will guard the eye to my last breath."

"Which you have just taken," the second count snarls, suddenly bursting with new power. He tosses Vystan aside easily.

You swing around. The second count's face contorts with fury. As you watch, he shimmers before your eyes. His azure cloak deepens to coal black. His face changes. His skin grows sallow, and his eyebrows thicken. His lips tighten to a cruel line, pale and scarlike. A thin, dark beard sprouts from his chin.

"Gorak!" he commands, raising his arms to cast a spell. Tyrion's voice has faded to a scratchy whisper that raises goose bumps on your arms.

The air around the evil wizard shimmers like heat. The hideous orog captain, chipped battle-axe in hand, appears at the wizard's side, along with a small band of orcs. They brandish short swords, halberds, pikes, maces, and spears. Their red eyes glare at you with a hunger for violence.

You yank out your long whip. Your companions leap to your side with their own weapons. Now you must protect the real Delwyn to keep the eye safe.

"I thought we were finished with all this!" Grigneth whines.

"Guards!" the real count shouts. A volley of arrows rains down from the parapet. One of the orcs shrieks, but you can't tell if it's from pain or battle-lust.

With bloodcurdling cries, the orcs swarm to attack, spreading across the courtyard. The count's guards draw their weapons. One group rushes down the winding stone staircase into the courtyard, while archers take up defensive positions to rain arrows down upon the enemy.

In seconds, Vystan, Beatrix, and the others have

formed a defensive knot around Count Delwyn and the Dragon's Eye. Snapping the air with the tip of your whip, you step in front of them and brace yourself as an orc with a huge mace lunges at you.

Turn to 35.

25

"I'll go with the escort group, sir," you say. "I'll do my best to see that the eye is delivered safely."

Fostyr nods and grins. "I'll go, too, sir." The wind blows his hair in a wild mass around his head.

You smile back at the whip-thin young man, relieved. You and Fostyr have been through so many campaigns together, it's hard to imagine him not guarding your back or you not guarding his. "When do we leave, sir?" you ask the captain.

"Immediately," he says, leading the two of you to the stairway. "Grigneth and the others are waiting at the south gate." He grips your arm. "I'm putting you in charge, Corlen. When you get to Crockport, take the Dragon's Eye to Count Delwyn's castle. Give it to no one but the count—he has the means to guard it properly—but beware of treachery. The legions of Iuz want this talisman badly. There's no telling what they might do to stop you." He sighs, and his twisted nose looks like the beak of a bird of prey. "Good luck."

"I presume you're staying behind to defend the tower," you say. "Good luck to you, too, sir. You have a lot of brave men and women behind you."

"Thanks," Captain Jongh says. "We'll need all the luck we can get. Now, get going before the orcs close off your escape!"

The captain pushes his way between the other fighters massing the walls. You take one last look at the approaching army. The orcs are close enough now that you can see their torches reflecting off their

battle-axes and halberds. You hear their heavy footsteps, the clank of their weapons and armor, their
snorting and grunting sounds of anticipation, the
creaking wheels of crude siege machinery, catapults
and battering rams. The battle for the tower is going
to be grim and bloody—but you and Fostyr have
another mission, a more important one.

You grit your teeth, then take the stairs two at a
time to catch up with Fostyr.

The courtyard is ablaze with torches in the gathering dusk. In the cool air, the smoke hangs low, making
the air bite as you breathe deeply.

You and Fostyr make your way across the teeming
courtyard to find the rest of your group. Fostyr leads,
winding through the chaos, and you follow him,
squeezing between knots of fighters struggling into
armor and sharpening blades and arrows.

You reach over your shoulder to feel in your quiver
and count the flint-tipped arrows. Thirty-eight. You
hope that will be enough. You glance at another stack
of arrows near one of the armory huts, thinking of
gathering a few more, but these are steel-tipped
arrows. Your curse makes them dangerous to use, and
you decide not to take the risk.

Near the south gate, the battle preparations are less
frantic, with fewer people running about. You catch
up with Fostyr, who has stopped in grim surpise, staring down at the fortress walls, where the body of the
spy who tried to desert lies, a deep red gash across his
throat.

"He deserved it," you say.

"I know," Fostyr agrees. "One traitor like that
could cause the whole tower to fall."

Stepping past the deserter's corpse, you and Fostyr
hurry to the south gate, where Grigneth is waiting
with the other fighters who have been selected. Grigneth has a tattered leather helmet and a bristly reddish beard. He had shaved his chin clean on his last
leave to Crockport, but now he has decided to grow

the beard back. His whiskers don't seem to be cooperating.

You see Beatrix, tall and broad-shouldered, her blonde hair falling in a tight braid down her back. She stands as straight as her lance. Vystan, jovial and barrel-chested, leans against the wall beside her, his flail held loosely in his hand. The grim-faced swordsman Peri is there, with his long black mustache like a dragon's tail. He is muttering something to Bresnor, who, sullen as usual, grunts and shrugs his longbow over his shoulder. Everyone is tense. It's a small group, but you respect the fighting ability of each member.

Near the water trough beside the gate, a string of horses, saddled and ready to go, stamp their hooves and whinny. You note with surprise that your horse and Fostyr's are already among them. Captain Jongh knows you better than you realized. He knew you'd choose to guard the eye.

You step up to the others. "Is everyone here?" you ask Grigneth, who nods in the affirmative. "Let's get going, then . . . no time to waste. I want—"

"Who put you in charge?" Grigneth demands, jutting his bristly chin forward.

"Captain Jongh," Fostyr says, stepping to your side.

A frown creases Peri's forehead. "The horses are a mistake," he says. "We need to travel quietly, slip through the forest unseen."

"We need to go quickly," you say, grasping your horse's reins.

Peri shakes his head. "They'll hear us. If we go on foot—"

"We need to go quickly," you repeat evenly.

Bresnor touches Peri's arm and gives him a warning look. Peri shakes off his grip, glaring at you.

You pretend to ignore him, but you are concerned about the dissent in your group. "Look, we already have enough problems with the orcs without fighting among ourselves. Enough is enough. Has anyone gone for provisions?" you ask.

Barrel-chested Vystan pats the nearest saddlebag. "The finest fare the Bloody Axe has to offer," he says.

"He means he got the stuff with only a few maggots," Beatrix says with a wink.

"I'm going to miss the maggots," Fostyr says, with a false sigh. "Especially the crunchy ones."

Everyone laughs nervously, which eases the tension. You glance at the south gate, wondering if you'll live long enough to eat again.

"Who has the eye?" Fostyr asks.

"I've got it," Grigneth says, pulling a leather thong around his neck. You see a large pouch before he drops the thong beneath his jerkin. He looks at you suspiciously, as if you are going to take it from him.

"Guard it well," you say, mounting your horse. You raise your head to shout at the guards by the reinforced wooden barricade. "Open the gate!"

The others in your party mount their own horses as two stout lancers strain to pull open the huge wooden doors. You cluck to your horse, calming the beast as it snorts and dances in place. "All right, we ride fast. Not a word until we're well away from the tower," you say, urging your horse toward the darkness beyond the gate. "I'll give the signal."

Fostyr and the others fall in behind you. The gate thumps shut, and the heavy crossbars slam into place. The finality of the sound causes a tingle along your spine. You are alone now, outside the protection of the fortress.

You touch your oaken sword and your bow for reassurance, then pat the coiled whip at your side, just to be certain it still hangs there. You feel confident in your skill with each of your weapons, as the orcs will discover if they challenge you.

As your little band moves at a steady trot away from the tower and into the tangled forest, you look back at the ramparts of Dragon's Eye Tower one last time. By the light of the rising moon behind the clouds, you catch a glimpse of the orc army approaching the earthen wall at the front of the tower, spreading out to surround it. Their battle cries shatter the night, growing louder and more fierce as arrows and pikes rain down on them from the ramparts. You turn away, urging your horse forward.

You and your group have gotten away just in time.

Go to 9.

26

Turning from the deadly rune-carved sword, you grab your whip with such force that you snap the thong attaching it to your belt. The whip uncoils like a snake in your hand.

"No!" you yell at Tyrion, cracking the whip.

Tyrion jerks his head in surprise. The sword against Fostyr's throat lets up a fraction of an inch.

In a fluid motion blurred by speed, you lash out with the supple weapon. The end of the whip wraps around the sword and Tyrion's hand. You yank the whip sharply, wrenching the sword from Fostyr's neck and Tyrion's grip.

Tyrion's wrist snaps loudly. His hand hangs at an odd angle. The rune-carved sword clatters to the ground even before the wizard can cry out in pain.

You jerk the whip free.

Tyrion screams and lunges for the sword, but Fostyr is quicker. Your friend dives to the ground, grabs the hilt of the sword, and snatches it up.

The orcs raise their weapons threateningly, bellowing battle cries. Tyrion backs away, glaring at you, his face stormy, his eyes filled with hatred.

"Come on, Tyrion!" Shouting with triumph, you crack the whip again. It flicks against the wizard's face, leaving a bloody cut on his left cheek, similar to the wounds he just inflicted on you with the tip of

your father's sword. Tyrion raises his uninjured hand and begins to work a spell.

An orc with a two-handed broadsword lunges at Fostyr. Fostyr raises the magical blade and slashes. The blade slices the orc's sword in half and slays the orc in the same motion.

Fostyr leaps toward Tyrion before the wizard can complete the spell. Tyrion stumbles back in sudden fear, shielding himself with both hands. His broken wrist makes one hand dangle at a sickening angle. The orcs freeze in their tracks, fearful of the enchanted blade, uncertain how to defend the wizard.

"Your turn to die, wizard!" Fostyr hisses, closing in for the kill.

Panic twists Tyrion's face. Though his broken wrist hangs useless, he manages to scrawl in the air with the fingers of his good hand, hastily weaving a spell.

Fostyr jabs the enchanted sword at the wizard, aiming for his heart.

You're blinded by an intense flash of light. Suddenly Tyrion's body is transformed into a purple-gray cloud of smoke. The smoke retains the shape of the wizard, but Tyrion himself is gone, transported to safety.

Fostyr thrusts the sword into Tyrion's smoky form, but the blade passes right through it. Seconds later, the smoke dissolves, leaving a foul stench in the air where Tyrion stood.

In fury, Fostyr slashes at the dissolving smoke with your father's sword, but his efforts are futile. "Coward!" Fostyr shouts.

A scream of dismay and anger erupts from the orcs, but before they can rally and attack you, a shower of arrows pelts them from the fringes of the woods. Six orcs sink to the ground.

You and Fostyr both dive to the earth to avoid being hit by another volley of arrows. "Who is it?" Fostyr asks.

"I don't know," you reply. "Friends, I think. They

seem to be shooting the orcs."

"For now," Fostyr says. But a moment later, he cheers as several archers step into view.

It's your companions. They must have decided to return and ambush the camp.

You leap to your feet, take up your whip, and charge the remaining orcs. With an explosive crack, your whip wraps around the neck of a large orc, one of Gorak's lieutenants. The braided leather strangles it, crushing its windpipe and leaving an ugly welt on the creature's gray-green skin.

Leaderless and confused, the orcs break ranks and flee into the surrounding forest. You hear them crash through the underbrush, howling in terror as if fiends are chasing them. Your comrades fire another volley of arrows at their backs as they retreat. Four more orcs fall. The only other sounds are the gurgles and moans of wounded orcs, growing quieter as they die.

The rest of your companions emerge completely from their hiding places in the trees, joining you in the empty camp. They look at you and Fostyr rather sheepishly. "We couldn't leave you behind."

"It sure sounded like it," you grumble.

"Hey," the flail wielder assures you. "It just took us a while to come up with a plan."

Fostyr clamps a hand on your shoulder. "Well done, my friend," he says gratefully.

You shake your head, uncertain. "But Tyrion escaped." And you're still cursed.

"At least, with Gorak dead and Tyrion gone, the orcs are without a leader for a while," Fostyr says.

You stop for a moment to consider, feeling the weight of the Dragon's Eye around your neck. For a few minutes, you'd forgotten about it. You grin, pulling the eye out from under your tunic. "I guess we can deliver this in safety now."

Fostyr smiles at you. "Not bad for a day's work!"

The End

27

Weary and discouraged, you try to forget this latest horror. Your companions stumble along behind you.

Your meager supplies of food are gone. You come across many lime-encrusted puddles, but the water is undrinkable. Your lips are dry and cracked from digging through the rubble after the cave in.

You have to find a way out soon, or you and your companions will die, lost in this endless maze. At least the Dragon's Eye will be buried with you. You smile with grim satisfaction at the thought of Tyrion screaming in rage when he discovers the eye has been lost once more.

"It's my turn to curse you this time, Tyrion," you say softly, chuckling to yourself.

Renda looks sidelong at you, as if you've lost your mind. You shrug and press on.

After several hours, you realize that you're hopelessly lost, but you dare not show it. You have passed so many caves and new tunnels that you can't remember if you've seen them before or not. They all look the same. You wonder what time it is. Days could pass and you'd never know it.

Several torches are starting to sputter. Without the torches, you're doomed. You order a few of them to be snuffed out, hoping to make them last longer. Relf continues to lead, carrying the brightest torch.

When you come to the next branching of tunnels, you call a halt. Everyone is exhausted; no one is thinking straight. You need your companions to be alert. You send Relf and the broad-shouldered soldier with the battle-axe to scout one branch of the tunnel.

"Report back in five minutes," you tell them.

Relf sighs deeply and heads off. You and Renda check the second tunnel.

Five minutes later, you and Renda rejoin Relf and the other soldier. Relf reports that their tunnel is partially caved in. "I don't want to take a chance on that one collapsing on us, too," he says.

"Fine with me," you say. "There's a place to rest up ahead in the other tunnel." The tunnel you and Renda took opens into a warm, dry chamber, large enough to hold everyone comfortably. You set up camp there.

To conserve torches, you put out all but the one the watch will use. Assigning Turloc the first watch, you curl up on the rocky cave floor. You roll part of your cloak under your head for a pillow, then pull a fold of it over you as a blanket, but the cave is still dank and cold. Luckily you're so tired it doesn't matter. You drift off to sleep, thinking that hard stone never felt so comfortable.

A faint singsong murmur awakens you. It seems to mingle with the snores of your companions. There's no light, not even from the watch's torch. The flail wielder must have let it burn out!

You move your fingers in front of your eyes, but you can't see them. You touch your face but still can't see your hands. The darkness around you is impenetrable. A chill spreads through you, raising goose bumps on your neck and arms.

"Turloc?" you whisper. "Turloc, you're supposed to be on watch!" No answer. You call louder. "Turloc!"

Nothing.

You wrap the cloak around you and feel your way to the wall. You hear the faint murmuring sound again . . . magical, lilting voices. Brushing your fingertips along the wall, you carefully place one foot in front of the other as you head down the corridor in the direction of the voices. "Turloc?" you call again.

Several minutes later, you round a corner in the passageway. Weak light flickers ahead. You creep toward it, like a moth to flame. Soon an arched doorway appears in the side of the tunnel. The voices seem to be coming from there.

"Power," they sing. "Riches. Land."

You approach cautiously, the words drawing you closer. Turloc stands as if hypnotized just inside the doorway. The torch hangs limply in his right hand. His eyes glint as he stares in awe.

"There you are, Turloc!" Relieved, you step through the doorway into a cavern dotted with glittering jewels: rubies, diamonds, emeralds, amethysts. Sapphires larger than your arm, gleaming opals like crystallized pure milk, tiger's eyes, garnets, every kind of gem you've ever imagined.

His mouth hanging open, the flail wielder stares at his left hand. It's filled with a rainbow of gems.

The singing changes, filling your ears.

> *"Hear the truth,*
> *or your heart's desire.*
> *Clearly see,*
> *or dream and expire."*

"Turloc," you say. You shake him, but he doesn't respond. It's obviously some kind of spell. Which did the stooped flail wielder choose, you wonder—truth, or desire? If you make the same choice, you'll end up the same way, transfixed and mindless.

You turn to get help, but you find you can't move. Your legs seem to be fastened to the floor. You can't get away. You must choose.

After a pause, you say aloud, "I choose to hear the truth. I want to see clearly." Maybe that will tell you how to free the flail wielder.

Within seconds, all the gems vanish and the singing turns to shrieks of fury. Instead of a vast cavern, you find yourself standing in a tiny cramped room chiseled out of rough stone.

Turloc clutches a few dirty pebbles in his hand. Skeletons of dwarves, orcs, and humans litter the floor, obviously those who chose their heart's desire and died, trapped by seeing only what they wanted and not what was really there.

You find you can move your legs now. Quickly you dump the pebbles from Turloc's hand. You drag him toward the door. He doesn't struggle, but seems limp, as if stunned.

The voices in the air shriek louder, buffeting you. Cries of misery chill you to the bone. Shivering, you stagger out into the passage.

As soon as you pass through the arch, the voices fade. Turloc shudders, looking up at you in confusion. The voices vanish.

"I heard . . . someone," he says, puzzled. "What happened?"

You explain the curse as you return to your companions. The flail wielder hangs his head, embarrassed.

"All those riches . . ." he says dreamily. "All I had to do was get out of these tunnels."

"We'll get out of the tunnels," you say, placing a hand on his shoulder. "Come on. Get some rest."

You wake Renda and ask her to take the next watch. You warn her about the voices.

By the time you settle down, the flail wielder is already snoring softly. You doze, starting awake when Turloc cries out suddenly. His eyes wide with fear, he turns to stare at you. "What if I don't wake up, Corlen?" he says. "What if I just keep on dreaming?"

"Dreams can't hurt you," you say. "It's only bad if you see nothing *but* dreams. You have to face reality."

He nods and closes his eyes, but his breathing is ragged for a long time. Finally it evens out into restful sleep. At last you can get some rest yourself.

Hours later, you wake refreshed. You light an extra torch and set out once more. Your head seems clearer now. The side passages and branchings in the main tunnel don't all look the same anymore. You wind your way through the labyrinth, choosing the passages that slope up—to the surface, you hope.

After an hour, the tunnel levels out. The walls are warm to the touch—almost hot. Small puddles of acrid-smelling liquid dot the floor. The odor makes your eyes water.

Squatting next to one puddle, you pull a thread from your cloak and dip it into the fluid. The thread sizzles and dissolves. Acid. Powerful acid.

Relf stands by your side, holding the torch at arm's length. Together you peer down the passage. The puddles of acid are far enough apart that you can avoid them if you're careful.

"Not much of a choice," Renda says.

You glance at the torches. They're almost burned out. You don't have much time to escape the caves.

"We can't go back," you say.

Go to 33.

28

You swing your bow toward Tyrion and aim carefully at the center of the eye. All along, you have known that your mission is the most important thing. You must not allow the evil sorcerer to possess the magical object, or he may crush thousands with his new powers. Even if it means the eye is destroyed . . . even if it means you will not be able to save Fostyr.

Tyrion grips the eye tightly, gazing into its petrified depths. A smile carves his lips as he stares into its night-black pupil. The sorcerer whispers faintly, speaking into its dark depths.

"'Two eyes from on high,'" he intones. "'One eye to see into the mind and heart. One eye to see the land below.'"

The ground begins to tremble. A shield with a coat of arms on the wall behind him clatters to the courtyard.

You take a deep breath and let your arrow fly.

The Dragon's Eye shatters in a flash of blazing light as its magic is released. A wave of heat passes over you, more intense than your father's forge on a blistering summer day. Tyrion shouts in surprise; then his shout becomes a scream of pain as the magical light engulfs him.

With a bellow of rage, Gorak draws the blade of an axe across Fostyr's exposed neck. You shout and run toward the orog, but your friend is already dead as Gorak drops him to the ground.

Tyrion cries out in pain as he frantically tries to work a spell. His hands are ablaze with the brilliant fire, and soon the glare ignites his entire body.

The orcs around him shrink back in terror. Vystan and Beatrix cover their eyes.

Tyrion's lips move, but the words come out slurred. His fingers wither. The flames consume his skin, and he sinks to the ground, as blackened and stiff as scorched tree limbs.

Inky smoke unfurls from his remains, stinging your eyes before the chill dawn breeze carries it away. In a fury, barely able to see from grief, you stagger toward Fostyr and his killer.

The clash of arms echoes over your hammering pulse as the surviving orcs continue to fight for their lives. You blink away the stinging smoke and gathering tears, glancing up in time to see Gorak rushing toward you, bloody battle-axe upraised. You raise your oaken sword just in time to deflect the downward slash of the axe.

The force of the blow wrenches the oaken blade from your hands, splitting it down the middle. You roll down and to the side. The axe blade clangs against the flagstones next to your head. Tiny needles of shattered stone prick the side of your face.

You roll again and heave yourself up to your knees, panting. Your wrist aches from the heavy blow that shattered your wooden sword.

Gorak looms over you, axe raised, face twisted in a snarl. You fumble for the whip at your side, but you know it won't be effective from a kneeling position.

Before you can move, Gorak's blade starts down.

Out of the corner of your eye, you see a blur of motion. Iron chains wrap around the orog's forearm. Vystan's spiked flail spins the huge orog around, yanking its blade arm wide.

Gorak howls in rage. The orog jerks its arm free, mindless of the tears the spikes make in its flesh. It rips the flail from Vystan's hands, knocking the portly fighter off balance and tripping him to the ground.

The distraction has given you enough time to get to your feet, however, and you unfurl the whip just as Gorak raises one iron-shod foot over Vystan's head. Vystan reaches up to grab Gorak's ankle and twists with all his might. Unbalanced, the orog jams its foot into Vystan's stomach, pinning him to the flagstones, and slashes sideways with the chipped axe. You lash out with your whip, catching Gorak in the face and slicing open a wicked gash on the monster's cheek.

Gorak's head jerks, as if it has suddenly remembered its real enemy. Vystan chokes and tries to knock the heavy monster off of his belly.

A scream of rage rings in your ears. Beatrix appears out of nowhere to land on the orog's back. She holds her dagger at Gorak's throat, but the creature gives one mighty shrug and sends her flying. She lands with a sickening thud and lies still, stunned.

Vystan manages to free himself during the distraction and rolls aside to grab for his discarded flail. He holds one hand over his stomach.

The orog turns on you, blinking to clear its vision from the sticky blood running down into its eyes. Beatrix rouses herself and thrusts at the creature with her lance, lodging its tip in Gorak's hip.

But Gorak, seemingly incapable of feeling pain, simply grabs the slippery shaft and tears it free, ramming the butt of the lance back into Beatrix's armored stomach. She stumbles and falls, the wind knocked out of her once more, but she manages to hold on to the lance. Seeing its helpless opponent, Gorak lunges

at her even as Vystan grabs his flail and comes charging toward the orog.

Looking up from the ground, Beatrix instinctively raises the tip of her lance. It pierces the orog's stomach as Gorak dives for her.

The monster's weight drives it onto the lance—and Beatrix. Beatrix cries out as the orog crashes down onto her. Something snaps in her chest. A last, smelly breath boils out of Gorak's mouth.

You rush to Beatrix's side and try to pull the orog off. Vystan helps you, heaving the orog general aside. The fighting around you dies into sudden silence. The rest of the orcs are dead. Beatrix's lips quiver, and she coughs, wincing with pain. You kneel beside her.

She moans, holding her hand to her side. "Tell me we won. I wouldn't want to have to put up with a set of broken ribs if we didn't."

You nod once and swallow. Vystan kneels at her side to tend to her wounds.

You stand. Yes, you've won. Tyrion can no longer threaten Furyondy. Neither can Gorak. They are gone, broken, along with the Dragon's Eye. Leaderless, the orc army will fall apart, with the defeated soldiers wandering back to Iuz or making new homes in some dark corner of the kingdom.

But Grigneth is dead, and Bresnor can no longer shoot his precious bow. Count Delwyn is dead, too, and the captain of the guard, and many other brave fighters lie strewn across the courtyard. As the day lightens, you can see more clearly how great the toll of this battle has been. The destruction of the eye carries a high price.

And Fostyr as well.

You walk over to where your friend's body lies sprawled on the ground, and you force yourself to look at him. Your lungs can't seem to draw in enough air to form the words you want to say.

It will have to be a silent good-bye.

Dazed, you walk out of the count's courtyard. As you trudge down the mountain to your home city of Crockport, you feel as if you, too, have died.

The End

29

You have fought too many battles and have too many regrets, but this time you refuse to stand by and let Fostyr die. Not without a fight. "Go, then," you tell the others. "I'm staying. All I ask is that you leave me one of your bows and some arrows."

You accept the bow and arrows from one of your companions before he disappears down the forest path. Then you nock an arrow and draw back your bowstring, aiming for Gorak. The orog raises its axe high above its head, and just as it tenses to deliver the death blow to Fostyr, you release the arrow.

The shaft sings through the air and buries itself in Gorak's neck. The huge orog stiffens and drops the axe at Fostyr's knees. Gorak raises both hands to the arrow, as if trying to tear it out. The orog's mouth opens, attempting to shout, but all that comes out is a choked gurgle before Gorak topples to the ground.

Fostyr jerks his head in your direction as battle cries erupt from the orcs. You nock another arrow, looking for Tyrion, but the wizard has disappeared in the sudden frenzy.

Instead, you drop an orc near Fostyr, hoping to give your young friend time to flee into the surrounding darkness. A red-eyed orc lunges toward him before he can escape. Grabbing Gorak's axe, Fostyr buries it in the orc's stomach.

Screaming for revenge, two huge orcs leap for Fostyr. You nock another arrow, take aim, and let fly. One of the orcs crumples, an arrow planted in its back. The second swings wildly at Fostyr with a flail. The rest of the orcs cluster together, shouting and challenging the darkness that surrounds their camp.

Reaching for another arrow, you find your quiver empty. You drop your bow and draw your oaken sword. If you can reach Fostyr in all the confusion, you might still have a chance to free him.

His back to the campfire, Fostyr hacks with the battle-axe at the shrieking orc. The monster staggers back, then rushes him, forcing Fostyr closer to the crackling campfire. The other orcs continue to bellow threats into the shadows.

A group of orcs heads for the forest a little to your right. You angle to the left, coming out of the brush near Fostyr. You keep low to the ground, trying to maintain the advantage of surprise.

As soon as you spring from the darkness, though, an orc spots you. It charges, spear held high. You deflect the blow with your wooden sword, then lunge in close, smashing the hilt into its piglike face. The cartilage in the creature's nose snaps with a crunch.

The orc staggers back, stunned. You rush past it, swinging your sword into the lower back of the flail-wielding orc threatening Fostyr.

The orc falls face first into the fire. Screaming, it rolls onto the ground, sending a fountain of sparks into the air. Its ragged fur garments burst into flames. The stench of burnt hair fills the air.

Fostyr glances at you with a broad grin, turning away in time to parry the slash of a short sword.

You ram your oaken blade into the ribs of the orc attacking Fostyr. You hear bones crack, and the orc gasps for air as it sinks to its knees.

"Follow me, Fostyr!" you cry, scanning the camp for an escape route.

Your friend joins you, guarding your flank. "It's no use, Corlen," he says.

The remaining orcs are converging on you, finally realizing there is only one attacker. They swarm toward you, weapons raised. A few of them laugh at the futility of your attack, while others howl in outrage. You grit your teeth. If you can only reach the forest, you and Fostyr might have a chance.

"This way," you say, motioning to the left.

You turn. Standing tall, holding the glowing magical sword, the wizard Tyrion stands between you and the cover of darkness.

"So it's you, Corlen," the wizard hisses. "Once a fool, always a fool. Considering my curse, I should think you'd know better than to become a fighter."

He repositions his hand on the hilt of your father's spell-engraved sword. Tyrion's raven's-head ring glitters in the firelight. The orcs drop back, sensing this isn't their fight.

"I should have killed you when I had the chance," Tyrion growls. "A mistake I won't make twice."

He strides toward you, the gleaming sword held out purposefully in front of him.

Turn to 39.

30

"We'll stay and fight the beetle," you say, raising Bresnor's bow. "It's the only chance we've got. This monster isn't simply going to let us float away."

Leaning over the side of the boat, you aim for the creature's head. You see the ripples of the water beetle's underwater passage making a wake on the lake's surface. You draw a deep, hissing breath. "Brace yourselves!" you warn.

Beatrix steps up beside you, her lance gripped tightly in both hands. Bresnor abandons his oar and takes up Peri's discarded sword. It looks heavy in his hand. The grim archer seems unaccustomed to holding a blade, but his concentration is focused entirely on the approaching monster.

When the beetle is about ten yards away, you let loose the arrow, hoping to hit the monster's mouth or even an eye. You doubt the sharp tip could pierce the giant insect's hard shell. The arrow ricochets off the beetle's carapace, splashing spray. The creature doesn't seem to notice at all. Its jointed legs stroke beneath the water, propelling it forward with increased speed.

"Move over," Beatrix says between gritted teeth. She hefts her lance. Before she can thrust it into the creature, the water beetle dives, vanishing underneath the boat.

Bresnor rushes to the other side, sword raised. Grigneth continues to hide at the bottom, whimpering, making the only sound on the boat. The lake falls still once more.

"Where is it?" you whisper. "Where did it go?"

A second later, the monster comes up under the boat, rocking it violently. You hear the waterlogged planks crack beneath you from the impact.

You fall to your knees. Beatrix grabs the boat's side to keep from falling overboard. Grigneth grunts as one oar swings to the side and knocks the wind out of him.

"Keep those oars in the water!" you shout to Vystan. "It'll help stabilize the boat. Grigneth, get up and help him!"

Breathless, Grigneth blinks his bloodshot eyes and climbs to the splintered seat. In terror, he hugs the handle of the oar to his chest. You nock another arrow, holding Bresnor's bow and swallowing hard, waiting for the next attack.

Beatrix looks around wildly. "Do you see it?"

Holding the other oar against his ample stomach, Vystan squints into the water.

"There! Behind you!" Bresnor shouts, whirling so hard that the boat rocks.

You turn toward the stern just as the beetle resurfaces, its mandibles clacking and its antennae thrashing from side to side like small, sharp whips. The attack is too sudden for either you or Beatrix to strike. The water beetle rams the boat, lifting the little vessel out of the water and spinning it around. The impact knocks you to the bottom of the boat. With its sharp, segmented foreclaws, the water beetle snaps off one of the planks from the side of the boat. It emits a high squeal, then drops beneath the lake again.

"Do something!" Grigneth yells. "Save us!"

Bresnor curses under his breath, leaning over the side of the boat with Peri's sword poised. Grigneth moans and hangs his head in his hands.

Your heart pounds in your chest as you shift to the opposite side of the boat. You can't kill the beetle if it stays underwater. You need to lure it close, to make it stay long enough for you or your companions to strike. Suddenly you have an idea. You hold out your hand to Beatrix. "Cut my hand," you say. "Make it bleed."

She stares at you, then nods as comprehension dawns. With a quick slice from her dagger, she opens a cut in your palm.

The wound burns like acid from the touch of metal

against your own cursed hand, but you pay no attention to that. As blood wells up, you hold your hand out over the water. Three drops fall like tears into the lake. The water boils as the beetle lunges for your hand, its mandibles spread wide.

You jerk your hand back suddenly. Beatrix aims for the heart of the monster's mouth and thrusts her sharpened lance toward the soft joints of its clacking mandibles, but the sharp lance deflects off the giant beetle's pincers.

Clutching at the side of the boat with its front legs, as if it means to tear the vessel apart plank by plank, the beetle slams its body against the boat. You scamper back, barely avoiding the slashing pincers. They snap shut on empty air.

Grigneth wrestles with the oar, his arms shaking uncontrollably. "I . . . I can't hold on much longer," he moans. "We're all going to die!"

Panting with exhaustion, Beatrix hisses at Grigneth, "If you don't keep quiet, we'll throw you overboard and escape while the bug eats you."

Bresnor raises the sword as the beetle rises up, rocking the boat, on the verge of capsizing it. He slashes wildly at the monster's head. The blade glances off the water beetle's shell, but with his second blow, the archer manages to sever one of the feathery antennae. "That's for Peri!"

Disoriented, the beetle squeals in pain and lunges again. You hear the sound of more planks cracking, and trickles of water rush in from the broken seams of the boat. You and your companions clutch at anything within reach to keep from being dumped into the water.

Bresnor strikes a third time with the heavy sword and finally succeeds in opening a small crack in the shiny black armor at the base of the beetle's head. Enraged, the beetle lunges at the archer.

With a shout, Beatrix jabs her lance into one of the beetle's eyes. Green ooze gushes out.

You stumble back from the creature, giving Beatrix room to manuever as she tugs her lance free.

"Come back, you coward!" she shouts as the beetle submerges.

With white knuckles, you clutch the pouch containing the Dragon's Eye. You wonder if it might have been better to stay at the tower and take your chances against the orcs.

Suddenly the oar is ripped from Grigneth's hands. He lunges for it, grabbing the handle as it slips under the lake's surface.

"No!" you shout. "Let it go!"

It's too late. The boat rocks precariously, and Grigneth tumbles overboard, sinking below a burst of churning bubbles. You see his hands thrashing about as he is attacked from beneath the murky water.

The boat shudders, rocking violently as water sprays over its side. Another large plank snaps in half, and streams of water flood into the boat. Vystan lurches forward, reaching out toward Bresnor to catch his balance. Thrashing and bellowing, the two of them tumble into the lake.

Surfacing once more, the voracious beetle skitters toward you, unable to see out of its wounded eye. Beatrix struggles to her feet as the boat begins to sink. Cold water gushes in from a dozen major leaks.

Beatrix raises her lance high, then jams it past the beetle's mandibles and down its yawning throat. A greenish trickle oozes from the beetle's mouth. The creature emits an ear-piercing screech. Twisting its unwieldy body, it knocks Beatrix aside and snaps the lance shaft before it slips under the surface, taking the embedded lance stump with it.

Trying to regain her balance, Beatrix grabs for you. Her fingers clutch the leather thong of the pouch around your neck. It breaks, and she plunges backward with a splash, dropping the eye. You make a grab for it as the boat plunges beneath the surface.

The beetle rises in front of you, dripping green

slime from its wounded eye and mouth, the broken lance stuck between its mandibles. One of its pincers closes around your thigh, dragging you under. With a surge of adrenaline, you wrench your leg free.

The monster attacks again as you desperately try to swim away. Finally, as you paddle backward, you kick hard and feel the sole of your boot strike squarely against the stump of the lance, driving it deeper, through the center of the insect's tiny brain. With a grunt and a convulsive jerk of all six legs, the beetle grows still in the water and begins to sink.

Then you remember the eye!

You spot Beatrix nearby and try to swim toward her. Taking a huge breath, you dive under the water.

The lake is clouded with bubbles and debris. You can see little as you swim down, down. Then you spot the pouch drifting past you, slipping toward the depths of the lake. You kick toward it, hands outstretched, but your hands close on water. Your burning lungs force you back to the surface.

Once back on the surface, you gulp down a big breath and dive again, swimming furiously to catch up to the slowly sinking pouch. You've got to recover the eye or your entire quest has failed. You glimpse the small, distant shape briefly before it vanishes into the deepening murk. You grope through the dark water until you can't stay down any longer. Your lungs are on fire. You surface and dive again.

It's useless. The pouch is gone.

You surface once more, shaking the water from your eyes. Something is floating on the surface about four yards from you. Your stomach curdles. It's what's left of Grigneth.

You realize that Grigneth's death may have been your salvation. While the beetle sucked him dry, it gave you and your companions just enough time to get ready for another attack. You take a deep breath and swim toward shore as fast as you can.

Soon you catch up to Beatrix. "Hurry," you gasp.

"We've got to get to shore. If there are any other beetles around, all the splashing and the blood will attract them."

Beatrix sucks in air. Vystan is just behind her, and he seems to be having difficulty swimming. The shore is a great distance away. Bresnor appears and helps Vystan, and you all swim toward shore together.

The ordeal seems endless, but finally your feet feel the muddy bottom of Lake Whyestil. You scramble to your feet and grab Beatrix by the arm, helping her ashore. Sputtering, Vystan also staggers ashore with Bresnor's aid. Together you slump onto the beach, miserable and staring out at the water.

Beatrix inhales deeply, then coughs and spits up a mouthful of water. "Do you still have the eye?"

"It's lost," you say, staring out over the water. "It's somewhere down at the bottom of the lake."

Bresnor hangs his head. "We've failed," he says hollowly.

But have we? you wonder. The eye is safe from the enemy's grasp. You can hardly think of a safer place. And your mission was to keep the Dragon's Eye from Iuz, wasn't it?

You shake your head and laugh bitterly. "Let's head for Crockport. Maybe we can at least get some dry clothes."

The End

31

Forgetting about Tyrion and the Dragon's Eye, you swing your bow toward Gorak and release the arrow. No matter what, you must save your friend.

The arrow whistles through the air and buries itself in the orog's throat. Gorak's mouth opens in surprise as much as pain, but no sound comes out. The orog drops Fostyr and clutches the arrow shaft, trying to yank it out of its thick, corded neck.

As soon as Fostyr hits the ground, his eyelids flutter and his eyes lose their glaze, taking on a startled look. He shakes his head, as if to clear it. As Gorak slides down the wall, still clutching at the arrow, Fostyr stumbles sideways.

The remaining orcs see their commander fall and wail in dismay, retreating toward the protection of the wizard. Vystan, Beatrix, and the count's remaining guards rush forward in a renewed attack.

Ignoring you and the rest of the battle, Tyrion grips the eye tightly. A smile carves his lips as he stares into the eye's night-black pupil. He whispers faintly into its dark depths. The air around him shimmers and crackles with swelling magical power.

"'Two eyes from on high,'" Tyrion intones. "'One eye to see into the mind and heart. One eye to see the land below.'"

The ground begins to tremble. A shield with a coat

of arms on the castle wall behind him clatters to the courtyard.

Frantically you search for another arrow—anything to prevent Tyrion from completing his spell and invoking the magic of the eye.

Nothing. You take out your oaken sword and race for Tyrion.

"Fostyr!" you shout. "Get Tyrion's sword!"

Your friend turns at the sound of your voice. When he sees you, some of his confusion seems to drop away.

The ground beneath the fortress shakes violently. You stumble and fall, then climb back to your feet. Fostyr looks around wildly, his gaze finally resting on Count Delwyn's body. He kneels beside the corpse, tugs the rune-carved blade free, and lifts the sword.

But not fast enough.

A stone topples from the wall behind you. The rumbling fills your head and rattles your teeth. The ground beneath the flagstones feels liquid.

You plant your feet wide, taking a deep breath, then hurl your oaken blade at Tyrion. The sword arcs end over end, then bursts into flame as it hits the shimmering air around the wizard and falls harmlessly to the ground.

Light bathes Tyrion's face. His hands jerk up protectively, shielding his eyes. He takes a step back, as if unsure of what he has unleashed.

The ground becomes still once more. Through the spots swimming across your eyes, you see Fostyr holding your father's sword in his hands.

Tyrion turns toward him, one hand raised to fend him off.

Fostyr strikes with the spell-enhanced blade. The sword slices into the wizard's chest. A cloud of putrid smoke roils out in great gouts, stinging your eyes and your throat. Tyrion sinks to the ground, as if a fire is hollowing out his insides. His arms and legs wither, consumed by the inner flames. When the fire reaches his face, Tyrion throws his head back and screams.

The cry pierces your ears with dagger sharpness. You clamp your hands to your head.

Suddenly the shriek stops and silence settles over the courtyard. The only sound you hear is the hammering of your heart. Your mouth is dry.

For a moment, no one moves. Then the count's guards rush the remaining demoralized orcs, dispatching them quickly with the help of Beatrix and Vystan. Others rush to help the wounded, including Bresnor, who is found unconscious by the wall where you left him. Someone shouts for healers to be sent up from the city.

You hurry over to Fostyr, staring down at Tyrion's charred remains. The Dragon's Eye is untouched by the flames of your father's sword. Its ice-black pupil peers up from Tyrion's blackened hand.

Fostyr smiles and claps you on the shoulder. You smile back, feeling as if he's returned from the dead. "Good work, Fostyr," you say.

"Thanks for snapping me out of it," he says. "I was trying to fight it inside my mind, but I couldn't break the spell."

This gives you an idea. With the wizard's death, you wonder if all of Tyrion's spells have been broken. You kneel and tentatively grasp the hilt of your father's sword, squeezing your eyes shut.

The metal sears your fingers. You quickly snatch your hand away. The curse has not died with Tyrion. You are still prevented from touching metal.

You stand and try to console yourself. Your father's death has been avenged. Tyrion is dead. The eye is safe, and so is the kingdom. And, after all, you haven't done so badly with a whip, a wooden sword, and your own wits.

The End

32

Your curiosity gets the best of you, and you decide to follow the stranger. Despite his marked stoop and furtive actions, there's something familiar about his face. An acquaintance from your early years in Crockport? you wonder.

"I'll be right back," you tell your comrades.

Vystan salutes you with his flagon. "We'll be here," he says. "As long as the ale and food last, we'll be happy to wait!"

Beatrix agrees with a long gulp from her own flagon. You wave to them distractedly and head for the back door of the inn. The mysterious man waits for you just outside the doorway. Motioning for you to keep quiet, he gestures for you to follow him. With a rapid step, he disappears into the shadows farther down the alley.

You hesitate. What if this is a trap? You immediately think of the Dragon's Eye hidden beneath your tunic. You should have left it in the protection of your friends.

The man slinks toward you along the back wall of the inn. You grip the hilt of your oaken sword.

"What do you want?" you ask.

The man shakes his head. "Not here," he says. "Too many people about. I can't risk anyone else hearing what I have to say."

From the other side of the brick wall, a group of merrymakers laughs raucously—loud enough to keep anyone from overhearing you if you speak quietly. "It's here or nowhere," you say, your boots planted firmly on the cobblestone alley.

The man glances about nervously, then heaves a long sigh. He leans close.

"Corlen, I knew your father before he died," the man says softly. "I visited him often, checking on swords commissioned for Count Delwyn's guard."

Your father's smithy . . . so that's where you've seen his face. This man worked for the count, paying your father in gold for each parcel of swords. In fact, when Tyrion killed your father with the rune-etched blade, you had started after him with a sword that had been commissioned by Count Delwyn to attack the wizard, but Tyrion worked his curse before you could strike.

"Pietr," you say. "That's your name, isn't it?"

The man smiles. "You have a good memory, Corlen." The smile fades. "Unfortunately I didn't come to reminisce."

"What is it you have to tell me?" you say, more curious now than ever.

Pietr leans closer. His breath is warm against your ear. "Do you have the eye with you?"

You stiffen.

"Don't worry," Pietr says. "I'm not here to take it. If that was my intent, I would have done so already."

A cough echoes farther down the alley, accompanied by a rattle of armor.

"Some of the count's guards," Pietr says. "They accompanied me to make certain we're not disturbed."

You relax a little. Captain Jongh charged you with delivering the Dragon's Eye to Count Delwyn. If Pietr is telling the truth, your quest could be over soon.

"Go on," you say.

"The count's castle has been infiltrated by Tyrion's spies. It's no longer secure. If you go there, the eye is almost certain to fall into the hands of Iuz. Count Delwyn himself barely escaped assasination. He's journeyed north toward Dragon's Eye Tower with the rest of his guards, hoping to intercept you before you arrive. Somehow you must have slipped past him."

"Where is he now?"

"Waiting for you at a secret camp in Vesve Forest. The guards know where to find him."

"You want me to go with them?" you say.

"You have to deliver the eye. The count can protect it."

"What about my companions?"

Pietr shakes his head. "They must not know of this. Because of Tyrion's spies, Count Delwyn trusts no one but his closest allies. He'll allow us to bring you to his hideout, but no one else."

You shift your feet uneasily. "But if I don't tell my companions I'm going, they're sure to look for me," you say. "That'll tip Tyrion off for sure."

Pietr glances back over his shoulder toward the guards hidden in the shadows as he considers your words. "All right," he says finally, "but you can't tell them where you're going."

You nod.

"I'll wait here for you," Pietr says. "Don't take long. Tyrion has spies everywhere."

You slip through the door of the Rusty Fishhook Inn and return to your companions. After several mugs of ale, they look even more relaxed. Half-empty tankards clutter the tabletop, and Vystan is on his second plate of food.

"Who was that?" Beatrix says, peering up at you over a forkful of mutton.

"An old friend of Fostyr's parents," you say, looking somber. "I'm going to visit them for a while and tell them about Fostyr. Get a room and catch up on rest. I'll meet you back here in the morning." That should buy you enough time to get away before Tyrion's spies notice you're missing.

Your companions become serious at the mention of Fostyr's name. "Tell them their son was a good friend," Bresnor says.

"And be sure they understand that he allowed himself to be taken so the rest of us could live," Vystan says.

"I will," you say, wishing you could do just that. After you deliver the eye, you promise yourself, then you can tell everyone what a sacrifice Fostyr made.

Outside in the alley again, Pietr stands next to the captain of the guards.

"You'd better go," Pietr says. "Good luck!"

"Aren't you coming?" you ask in surprise.

Pietr shakes his head. "Like your friends, I must stay behind to keep up appearances and also to keep the count advised of the situation. Now I must return to the castle."

"We're wasting time," the guard says. He lurches off, and you follow. After several seconds, you glance back, but your father's friend has already vanished into the shadows. You wonder if you'll ever see him again.

At the end of the alley, you meet up with the rest of the guards—seven heavily armed soldiers. They lead you through the back streets of Crockport, coming out along the western shore of Whyestil Lake and the docks near where your little boat is tied.

Soon you enter Vesve Forest, tramping along one of the narrow paths under the trees, and the lights of Crockport disappear behind you. You and your companions head quickly northward, the responsibility of delivering the eye safely urging you on as fast as you can go.

Turn to 10.

33

You step over a small pool of acid.

The fumes are so strong you can taste them. The inside of your mouth feels as if it's on fire. Your eyes water. Your throat is a raw blister, and your lungs hurt. After only a short distance, it becomes impossible to speak. The others are coughing and wiping their eyes. You try to breathe through your nose, but the burning stench assaults your nostrils.

You pull a corner of your cloak over your nose, mouth, and ears. Except for your eyes, the burning eases somewhat. Your comrades follow your example.

Their coughing diminishes as they trudge forward.

After about a hundred yards, the puddles grow less frequent and smaller. The air clears, and you feel a faint breeze from above. Your eyes continue to water, but the stinging eases. Your lungs start to clear.

The acid fumes have parched your mouth, and your tongue is cracked and swollen. But in your entire party, only a few sips of water remain.

You study the walls around you. The tunnel is unnaturally glassy and smooth. Maybe miners cut it, using the acid. If so, you might be close to the surface. You hope so.

You hurry on. A second tunnel angles off to the left. Rougher and less even, this one has no pools of acid. The air smells fresher. With a sigh of relief, you unwrap the cloak from your face. Motioning to your group, you set off down the new passage.

Finally you seem to be getting somewhere. The tunnel floor slopes steadily upward, past many smaller caves and tunnels. You push on, tired, but too excited to stop and rest. Your long underground journey could finally be over.

"Spread out!" you say. "Look for a way out!"

Everyone heads off in different directions. You enter a tiny chamber filled with rubble. Backing out, you move on to the next cavern. Although much larger, this one is no more helpful than the first. You enter a third chamber. Little more than a narrow hallway blocked by a giant slab of rock, it doesn't seem to have a ceiling. Curious, you raise your torch.

Hundreds of fluttering black wings swoop down, shrieking at the upper range of your hearing. You thrash your arms, protecting your eyes as bats flap around your head and shoulders. You swing your torch like a club, stunning several bats and knocking them to the floor of the cave. You run, retracing your steps.

The bats vanish into blackness. Panting for breath, you watch their flight. There must be a way out nearby.

Encouraged, you rush into the next cave. Foul air assaults your nose. You gag on the stench of rotting flesh.

Not only does the chamber reek, but its shape reminds you of an eye socket in a human skull. Raising your torch, you look around. Manacles hang from the walls. Torn, bloody clothing and a shield lie on the floor beneath the wrist irons. Bones litter the ground beneath three unlit torches.

You remove one of the torches and light it from the stub of your torch. The hair on the back of your neck prickles. Fostyr told you that chambers like this riddle these tunnels, each guarded by some unknown monster.

You start to back out, then stop. No one would willingly enter such a cave. Perhaps you should hide the Dragon's Eye here, where the monster that rules this horror chamber can guard it. Then maybe the wars and the killing would stop. People like Fostyr will no longer have to die. You grit your teeth and creep into the room, looking for a good place to conceal the eye.

A bone snaps underfoot. Fear spikes through you. You take another step. Another bone snaps, as if cracked by jaws.

You halt. Something is watching you. You can feel its gaze in the dark. Your heart pounds. You back up slowly. Cold sweat chills the back of your neck.

Someone shouts from one of the other caves. You dash out of the chamber, dropping the newfound torch. Your shoulder blades tense, awaiting some kind of attack.

Nothing snares you.

Another shout echoes through the caves.

You run toward the voice, loosening your oaken sword as you go. Light flickers around a big outcropping of stone. Your companions are gathered around Relf.

"What's going on?" you say, gasping for breath.

A pike carrier steps aside, letting you squeeze in beside her. Turloc kneels beside another pale soldier. He holds the soldier's right hand, examining it.

The pale soldier looks up at you. "I burned myself exploring a tunnel."

"How is his hand?" you ask the flail wielder.

He grunts and frowns. "It'll heal," he says. "There are only a few blisters. I wish we had some cold water we could soak it in."

"I'll be okay," the soldier says.

"Where's the tunnel where you hurt your hand?" you ask.

"In the next cave," the soldier says, climbing to his feet. "I'll show you."

Cradling his burned hand against his chest, he leads you to the tunnel.

The reek of acid hits you before you reach the opening. You hold out your torch and walk slowly down the passage, Renda at your side. The tunnel comes to a dead end after several yards. The rock wall in front of you is cracked and soft-looking, like strange, warm clay.

Renda pokes at it with her torch.

The rock shifts suddenly, then rumbles toward you. You back up quickly, fearing another cave collapse.

The oozing rock follows you out of the tunnel and into the cave, like a wad of mobile mud.

"It's alive!" the pale soldier shouts, scampering out of the way with the rest of you.

The thing stops just outside the tunnel opening. It looks like a huge stone slug. It reeks of acid. It rears up, looming large in the dimness.

Renda inhales sharply. "A horgar," she says. "I should have known."

You back away, recalling how the creature can burrow through solid rock with its acid.

Turloc swears softly under his breath.

The horgar scuttles toward Relf, forcing him back against the cave wall, then hesitates. "Help!" Relf shouts, looking frantically toward his sister.

You stiffen. The horgar might leave Relf alone if you don't provoke it. But it might also attack him. Renda looks desperately toward you.

Should you attack the creature first?

If you attack the horgar, turn to 12.
If you decide not to attack the horgar, go to 6.

34

"I'm staying," you say, unconsciously fingering the Dragon's Eye hidden beneath your jerkin. You have given your word to Captain Jongh, and you refuse to take the coward's way out.

Alix scowls at you. "Die if you want to," he says, then slips away.

A few moments later, Fostyr hurries up the stairs with a muffled clatter, carrying a huge crossbow. The steel bolts it fires are heavy enough to punch holes in the best metal armor. "Something to keep the orcs occupied," he says, grinning at you.

"Just in time," you say, nodding to a fiery line that marks the edge of the orc encampment. "It looks as if they've had enough waiting." The torches are beginning to advance toward the tower like a stream of falling stars.

"Okay," Fostyr says. "This is it!"

With a pounding heart, you unsling your longbow and take your position at the battlements. The other archers take their positions, strung out on either side of you. Those with crossbows kneel in front, making it easier for you to shoot over them. Fostyr braces his crossbow on a gap in the wall's crenellations, squinting toward the advancing army, selecting his target.

One of the captains marches up and down the walkway, shouting orders to the tense defenders. "Wait till they get close enough! Don't waste a shot;

we need to make every arrow and bolt count."

You see four gaps in the line of fighters along the wall. You glower. Gaps created by the deserters.

Standing firm directly behind Fostyr, you nock an arrow. Your pulse is hammering. You hear other fighters cough nervously, shifting from foot to foot. Fostyr looks up at you, and you nod in silent acknowledgment.

Below, you can hear the clanking footsteps, the rustling weapons, and the harsh guttural cries of the battle-hungry orcs. Shouts of alarm and challenge come from the earthen perimeter wall. The flames under the cauldrons of boiling oil are stoked higher.

Finally the waiting is over. Drawing a deep breath, you steady yourself. The odor of hot oil singes the inside of your nose and lungs.

"Longbows first," the captain says. "Wait until you can see the reds of their eyes."

"Won't be hard to hit 'em if they stay in a group like that," an archer named Renda says, readying her bow. Her hair glows copper in the moonlight.

"Maybe we should thank them for doing us a favor," her twin brother Relf says, nudging her with his elbow.

The other defenders around you laugh nervously, breaking some of the tension. In the forest outside the tower, the orcs advance in a ragged line beneath the pale underbelly of the moonlit clouds, marching to a pounding, intense drumbeat. In the middle of the orc army, a tattered, dark standard whips violently in the cold breeze from the lake. The orcs swarm past the banner, like lightning around the calm eye of a hurricane.

Two riders mounted on huge black horses follow the flag bearer—an orog general, larger and more hideous than a common orc, and a smaller figure who seems to be its master. They ride confidently out in the open, as if they have nothing to fear, as if the battle is already won. Anger boils in your veins. They won't be so confident once they get into range.

"They have a wizard with them," Fostyr mutters under his breath, so low that you can barely hear him.

But there's no time to ask about the wizard. The ranks of the orcs break spontaneously, and the monsters rush forward, screaming and waving their weapons in a stampede to the tower.

Battle cries of the orcs buffet you, a roar from the brewing storm. They are close now, less than two hundred yards away. You draw your bowstring back, savoring the strength and tension in the weapon. The bow feels like a living animal, the arrow a tethered falcon waiting to be released.

"Now!" the captain shouts.

An arrow pierces the night. Then a wave of arrows fall like razor-edged rain from the clouds. You are tempted to shoot at the swollen orc commander, but decide instead on a group of soldiers closer to the wall, where your arrows have a better chance of striking home.

Screams punctuate the battle cries of the orcs as thirty or more of them fall under the deadly first volley of arrows. Arrows from orc archers clatter against the wall of the tower. A man behind you grunts, then falls to his knees, clutching a crossbow bolt in his chest. The twin archers, Relf and Renda, move in unison to haul him aside, yelling for a healer as they return to their stations and launch their counterattack.

You nock another arrow, then another and another until, all too soon, your quiver is empty. You glance around frantically. At least five archers have fallen along the wall, not counting the deserters. A great many more orcs lie strewn on the battlefield around Dragon's Eye Tower, thank the gods. But they had a lot more soldiers to start with.

Below, on the earthen perimeter walls, fighters work together to tip over the huge black caldrons, spilling the steaming oil down onto the swarms of orcs scrambling up the walls. With shrieks of pain, the burned monsters try to retreat, but the press of the rest of the army pushes them up against the packed earth, trampling them underfoot. More boiling oil pours down, causing vast numbers of casualties, but still the orcs keep coming.

A wide-eyed, pasty-faced stableboy thrusts a bundle of arrows at you. "Here!" he shouts, then moves on to supply another archer, gathering up black orc arrows that lie scattered on the flagstones.

Sweat trickles down the side of your face. Your lips taste salty and your hands are slick. You ignore your aching fingers and nock one of the new arrows.

So many dead orcs litter the base of the earthen wall now that the rest are having a hard time climbing over them. It slows them down, making them easy targets. But if the bodies keep piling up, the orcs will have a ramp formed from their own fallen comrades.

After you and the other archers have picked off several dozen more, the orcs finally seem to realize their vulnerability and retreat, leaving a mass of dead and dying monsters in their wake. A loud but weary cheer goes up from the fighters around you. A second cheer rises from the courtyard below.

"It's not over yet," Fostyr says, panting heavily.

Together you and your friend sink down behind the wall and struggle to catch your breath. You lean your head against the rough stone.

"How soon before they attack again, do you think?" you ask, peering through the opening in the wall next to you. With a sinking heart, you see the orcs already rapidly regrouping, terrified by the bellowing voice of the huge orog commander and his wizard master.

Fostyr shakes his head. "Don't plan on getting any sleep."

"I just hope I have time to get a few more arrows." You look around for the stableboy. "I don't suppose the fighters on the perimeter wall can boil any more oil."

Fostyr shakes his head, then takes a sip of water

from a nearby skin, passing it on to another archer. "I think the first round depleted all our stores."

You look at the bodies strewn around you. You count eleven. How many more are wounded?

"Look!" Renda cries suddenly, leaping to her feet as Relf stands beside her.

Wearily you struggle to your knees. Your arms and legs throb. The fingers of your bowstring hand are so stiff you can barely move them. You felt better before the brief respite.

The orog commander and the wizard ride forward a short distance as the cowed orc army peels back to let them pass. Side by side, the two leaders come to a stop. The orcs close in behind them, like a wound sealing itself. A deathly silence falls over the battlefield, shattered only by the sound of the wind whipping from the lake.

The stableboy stops filling quivers. "I don't like the looks of this," he says.

"Me neither," Fostyr says.

"They're in range," you say optimistically, lifting your bow, hoping to take one or both of them out.

Fostyr puts a restraining hand on your arm. "Don't waste your arrows. They'll never reach them." Fostyr smiles grimly. "Not unless you have a few magic spells tucked up your sleeve you haven't told me about."

No, you think bitterly. The only magic spell up your sleeve is a curse.

A gust of chill wind batters the tower, hard enough to make the ancient stones tremble.

"I really don't like this," Relf says.

The wizard raises his hands, slashing with his fingers and carving glyphs in the air.

"The ground is shaking," Renda says, looking down at her feet.

The tower rumbles underfoot with a tired, age-old moan, as if the earth itself is stirring from a deep sleep. A section of the perimeter wall at the foot of the tower bulges upward into an earthen mound. Three long cracks form on the top, radiating down from a knobby ridge.

"What is it?" Fostyr asks, trying to see. In a few moments, the shape becomes recognizable.

"It . . . it looks like a hand," you say in disbelief. "A giant hand made out of dirt."

The tower shifts sickeningly. You stagger to one side, bracing yourself against the stone wall with both hands. The jagged outline of knuckles and fingers sharpens on the earthen monstrosity, rising up in the shape of a clenched fist, ready to strike.

Captain Jongh appears at the top of the stairs, his broken nose forming a short, sharp zigzag on his face. "Quick, everyone down to the courtyard," he shouts over the deafening rumble. "We'll make our stand there."

"What about the tower?" Renda asks.

"The tower is lost," Captain Jongh replies grimly. "So is anyone who stays up here." He flashes a meaningful glance at you, and you know he is thinking about the eye hidden beneath your jerkin. You wonder if the decoy group is safe or if they've already been captured.

Loose rocks tumble from the knuckles of the giant earthen fist. Dirt pours off the thumb and fingers as it continues to rise from the ground, like a waking giant reaching for the sky. A network of tree roots holds the hand together like tendons in living flesh.

"Corlen," Fostyr yells. "Hurry, let's go!"

You glance over your shoulder. The orcs are already shouting in anticipation, bloodthirsty screams as dark and foul as the smoke from the torches they carry. They rattle their spears against shields.

As you turn to run, you notice something on one of the rocky fingers of the mammoth fist. The image of a ring, made of pebbles and stones, encircles one finger, its emblem carved deep into its rocky face. You stare in horror. The ring bears a raven's head.

Your pulse quickens as the meaning becomes plain.

The wizard is Tyrion.

Tyrion sits astride his black horse, his own clenched hand raised, as if puppeting the motions of his sorcerous giant fist. He strikes at the air, pretending to deliver a heavy blow.

At the tower's perimeter wall, the dirt fist moves forward across the courtyard, uprooting flagstones and smashing small structures aside. As you watch in awe, the stables and the old inn collapse.

Picking up speed, the mammoth fist smashes into the side of the tower itself, even as you and your companions flee down the swaying stairs. Heavy stone blocks topple from the parapet, jarred loose by the blow.

You lose your balance, then stumble down the remaining stairs where Fostyr waits. Dragon's Eye Tower shudders as you leap out into the open courtyard, your heart pounding wildly. You try to get away from the falling stones. A second blow from the sorcerous fist shakes the tower.

Rubble crashes behind you as the centuries-old Dragon's Eye Tower collapses in a cloud of dust.

Turn to 14.

35

The orc swings its mace mightily in a huge arc. With your other hand, you draw your oaken sword and parry the blow, smashing the orc's fingers. The orc bellows, and the spiked mace clangs to the ground, giving you the opening you need to thrust the hardened point of your sword into the hollow of the orc's scaly throat. The creature staggers back and collapses.

Beside you, Bresnor grunts in pain. You turn as an orc yanks its battle-axe free from a deep gash in Bresnor's upraised right arm. Grinning, the orc swings again. Bresnor tries to block the attack with his splintered longbow, but the orc's axe slices through the bow like paper and lops off Bresnor's arm just below the elbow. Bresnor falls to his knees, clutching at the wound, trying to stanch the flow of blood. His face is grayish and wet with shock.

You snap your whip around the orc's throat, winding it tightly like a garrote. You let your outrage flow as you jerk back the whip, snapping the orc's neck.

Letting the creature's body fall, you grab the collar of Bresnor's leather jerkin with one hand and drag him from the fray toward the nearest wall of Delwyn's fortress. The archer's eyes are glazed with shock, and his body trembles as you prop him against the wall.

"Hang on," you say. Setting down your wooden sword, you rip the sleeve from your cotton shirt. You kneel and bind the cloth as tightly as you can around what's left of Bresnor's forearm. The blood slows to a dribble as you tie the knot tight. You hope it will be enough. Bresnor gasps, then weakly pushes you aside.

"Go help the others. Leave me. You can't let someone else die while you play nursemaid with me."

"You'll be all right," you say, rising to your feet.

"Not if you let those orcs win."

As you turn, an orc wielding a short sword charges you from the melee. You drop to your knees, ducking your head as the orc's wild slash singes your hair. You swing your sword into the side of the orc's knee, chopping with the hard wood. You hear the sound of bone snapping and cartiledge tearing. The orc tumbles to the ground with a howl. You smash its neck with another blow.

Panting and sweating, deafened by the sounds of the raging battle, you look up quickly. A dwindling knot of guards surrounds the real Count Delwyn and Fostyr. The bright red blood of fallen guards mixes with the darker, thicker blood of the orcs on the flagstones.

Cut off from the count, Vystan, Beatrix, and Grigneth are backed against the far wall in a tight defensive triad. Dead orcs lie scattered around them. Grigneth has lost his leather helmet, but he is fighting furiously, with the strength born of terror. Vystan's chain mail is coated with gore. Beatrix's lance jabs in and out as quickly and deftly as a serpent's tongue, tasting blood with each thrust.

Beyond the edge of the fray, Tyrion and the orc commander, Gorak, stand at a safe distance, watching the battle. For a moment, your eyes lock on Tyrion's. He smiles at you, the same thin sneer you remember after he killed your father.

It's as if history is repeating itself, only this time he will kill Fostyr, and your companions, and take the eye for himself in the aftermath of the battle. No, you tell yourself. It must not be!

You stagger to your feet, lurching in the direction of Tyrion and Gorak. You clasp the wooden sword in one hand and your whip in the other. Tyrion waits for you, smiling, egging you on.

An orc with a bloody-tipped spear steps in your path. Several of its yellowed front teeth have been knocked out, but the orc doesn't seem to notice.

You deflect its thrust with your sword, making a sound of hard wood clacking against wood. Without a pause, you move in close, slamming the hilt of your sword into its chest, hearing the hollow crack of its sternum. The orc staggers back and trips over one of Delwyn's fallen guards. The creature tumbles backward onto the ground. Before it can rise to its feet, you leap on it, crushing its windpipe with your knee.

Now it's time to face Tyrion.

To your left, an orc with a two-handed sword hacks at Grigneth. Using a short sword, he parries the attack—just barely. Fatigue and fear line his face. The blade nicks Grigneth's cheek, and a thin line of blood trickles down into his beard stubble.

You rush to help him. Desperate, Grigneth lunges for the orc's throat with his short sword. The orc blocks the attack easily, then twists its sword down, plunging it deep into Grigneth's belly.

You can almost feel his muscles rip and tear as if they were your own. Grigneth might have had a streak of cowardice in him, but he fought well at the end. The man moans and slumps to the ground, a death rattle in his throat.

Before the murderous orc can shout its triumph, you leap behind it, raising your sword to bring it down on the back of the orc's skull. At the same time, from the opposite side, Vystan's flail catches the orc in the face. The orc's head snaps back; it falls dead before it can make another sound.

Beatrix yanks her long lance from an orc's chest and crouches, thrashing her head. Her blonde braid flips from side to side like a pendulum.

You turn, expecting another attack, but the three of you are alone. Only nine orcs remain, and they are engaged with the count's guards.

With Vystan and Beatrix beside you, you rush to

help the beleaguered humans just as Gorak steps forward to hurl a feathered spear. Its wide triangular tip catches Delwyn's captain of the guard full in the chest. He stands for a moment, clawing at the shaft, then shudders and falls forward. The shaft of the spear snaps as the captain collapses onto it.

With renewed confidence, the orcs surrounding the count let out a howl. They attack with a frenzy, pinning the count's guards against the castle wall.

Vystan hurls himself at one of the orcs, blindsiding it with his deadly flail. Beatrix wades in after him, plunging her lance into the exposed back of an orc as if she were skewering meat on a stick.

You run to head off Gorak, the orog commander. But before you can reach the massive general, Gorak charges through the defenders, cutting a path to the count with its battle-axe. Looking triumphant, Tyrion follows close behind, his rune-engraved sword raised in front of him.

Count Delwyn still holds the pouch with the eye, protecting it with his life, as he had promised. No slouch of a warrior himself, the count slashes at Gorak, ducking a vicious swipe from the orog's battle-axe. Fostyr stands motionless nearby, still trapped in the spell, his back pressed against the wall.

There's no way you can reach the count or Fostyr through the press of monster warriors. You look around the trampled courtyard and spot a longbow, dropped by one of the archers who died on the parapet. Sheathing your oaken sword, you run for the bow, wresting it from the archer's dead hands. Moving swiftly, you bend down to yank an arrow from the body of a fallen orc. A single arrow. You will have one shot only.

You swing around. One of the count's guards is trying to fend off Gorak with a spear. You nock the arrow and draw back the bowstring, aiming at Tyrion. Hatred and vengeance blurs your vision. But Tyrion is engaged with Count Delwyn, pressing close. You wait for a clear opening, afraid of hitting the wrong person.

The count swings his long sword at Tyrion's neck. The wizard, drawing skill from the magical runes your own father carved into the sword, parries the blow easily.

The count's next thrust is aimed at the wizard's heart. Tyrion swats the thrust aside. At the edge of the skirmish, the purplish-faced Gorak strides toward the blank-eyed Fostyr. The orog raises its battle-axe, seeing an easy target.

You spin around with the bow and take aim on a new target.

With one arm, Gorak lifts Fostyr by the waist. The orog turns to face you, pressing the blade of its axe against Fostyr's throat. It seems to be taunting you. You draw the bow back as far as you can, praying no one steps in the way.

Gorak hesitates, glaring at you as a flurry of other fighters comes between you and the orog. Your fingers ache and your lungs burn. You curse the guards and orcs blocking your shot.

"Move out of the way!" you shout in frustration.

At that moment, Tyrion raises his sword. He slashes down. The count shifts his long sword to block it, but Tyrion's spellbound blade slices it in two and continues its downward sweep without slowing. Tyrion's sword slices deep into the count's neck, all the way to the bone.

The count stumbles backward, already dead. The Dragon's Eye tumbles out of the leather pouch and begins to fall.

"No!" Tyrion shrieks. He drops his sword and lunges for the falling eye before it can shatter on the flagstones. He shoves the count's limp form aside and leaps for the falling talisman.

Tyrion stands, clutching the unbroken eye in his hands. He holds it high above his head, a smile on his face and a shout of triumph escaping from his lips.

Gorak sneers, pressing the battle-axe deeper into

the hollow of Fostyr's throat.

You swallow. You have only one arrow. Whom do you shoot? Gorak, before it kills your friend? Or Tyrion, who now has the all-powerful eye?

Though the arrow might not harm Tyrion, it might smash the eye and keep him—or anyone—from using it.

You take a deep breath and let it out slowly. Your arms tremble with tension. Your aim must be perfect.

Do you save Fostyr and risk tipping the balance of power between Furyondy and Iuz in Tyrion's favor? Or do you destroy the eye and save the land, knowing you will be haunted for the rest of your life by the fact that you could have stopped Gorak from slitting your friend's throat?

If you choose to aim for the Dragon's Eye, turn to 28.

If you choose to aim for Gorak, go to 31.

36

"I'm staying here, Fostyr. I won't leave you to face all these orcs alone." You uncoil your whip and crack it at the snarling orcs.

You look around at the scattered pockets of defenders fighting their way toward the tunnel opening. "Go on!" you shout to them. "Hurry!"

Even though the opening is partially encircled by the collapsed wall of Dragon's Eye Tower, you realize it will take more than one person to keep the tunnel stairs open long enough for everyone else to escape.

"I'll watch your back," you say. Before Fostyr can protest, you climb a pile of stones behind him, joining the few last fighters struggling to hold back the advancing tide of orcs. Your whip cracks repeatedly. Someone has jammed torches along the outer edge of the collapsed wall. They cast enough light for you to see and provide a barrier of flame. You snatch up a torch in your other hand and wave the burning end in the faces of the orcs.

The creatures press in from all sides. The broken boulders remaining from the tower wall rise about six feet above the surrounding rubble. The tumbled broken rocks and the upthrust flagstones of the courtyard slow the flood of orcs, but it's only a matter of time before they overrun your position. With luck, you and Fostyr will be able to retreat down the tunnel stairs after the others and continue the fight there.

You lash out again at the orcs reaching up at you, blinding two of them. Casting aside the torch, you draw your wooden sword. Then, whip in one hand and sword in the other, you run along the top of the wall to the next group of weary defenders, thrusting and stabbing with spears and swords. You recognize the twins, Relf and Renda. "Head for the tunnels!" you shout at them. "We'll have a better chance down there."

"What about you?" Renda asks. She grunts, jabbing her spear at an orc trying to climb the wall. The orc screams, clutching its mouth, then falls to the rubble below.

"I'll follow in a minute," you say. "I'm staying to help Fostyr."

Renda nods. "Good luck." She grabs her brother by the arm, and they skitter down the broken boulders behind you toward Fostyr and the tunnel entrance. Without hesitating, they grab up torches, duck their heads, and hurry down into the winding underground passages.

A small orc crawls over the lip of the wall to your left. It curls its lips back in a snarl, revealing blood-splattered teeth, and it thrusts at you with a short sword. You swing the heavy blade of your wooden sword down on its wrist, snapping the creature's thin bones. The attacker's sword clatters to the top of the wall. You kick the orc in the face, and it falls back into the darkness, gurgling.

You glance around quickly. Except for orcs, the top of the wall is empty. So is the courtyard. Your comrades are either dead or making their way into the tunnels. Fostyr is single-handedly battling a cluster of orcs as the last group of defenders stumbles past him to the tunnel stairs.

Good. In a couple of minutes, they'll all be protected. You can get the eye to safety.

Five or six orcs crawl onto the top of the wall to your right, knocking the torches aside. It's a good thing the wall is narrow, you think. They can only attack you one at a time. You lash out at them with your whip. They advance toward you slowly, brandishing their swords in front of them to deflect the lashes from your whip.

A metal-tipped arrow from below nicks your arm, opening a deep cut. The wound burns like molten iron. You grit your teeth against the pain, whirling to find this new attacker.

A second group of orcs climbs up onto the wall behind you. The leader loads a bolt into its crossbow and takes aim at you. Without time to think, you throw yourself facedown onto the top of the wall at the same instant the orc fires. The crossbow bolt whistles over your head. A shrill scream erupts behind you as the bolt strikes another orc. You leap to your feet as the dying orc topples from the wall.

The fallen orc's companions bellow at it and shove the dying body out of the way. You grab a torch at your feet and hurl it at your attackers. An orc deflects the torch with its sword. A shower of burning embers scatters on the night wind.

"No kill him," one of the orcs orders. "Gorak want prisoners."

The two groups of orcs advance slowly, closing in on you from both sides. You lash out savagely with your whip. If you can only drive them back a few steps, you might gain enough time to leap down to Fostyr.

You wipe at the sweat pouring into your eyes. The stench of the orcs is overpowering. Out of the corner of your eye, you see Fostyr surrounded by howling orcs. You turn to him, ready to rush to his aid, when something strikes you on the back of the head. The blow stuns you. Black spots dance behind your eyes, and you fall under the crushing weight of the oncoming enemy soldiers. . . .

* * * * *

When you regain consciousness, your head throbs as if metal-shod orcs were dancing on top of your skull. Squirming, struggling to sit up, you find you are lying on your side on cold, trampled ground. Your hands and feet are bound with biting leather thongs that cut into your wrists and ankles. Your bones ache, and your muscles are so stiff you feel like a mummy. Slowly you open your eyes.

Firelight licks at your vision, bright tongues of flame that illuminate tents and a small pile of scavenged, blood-encrusted armor and weapons that haven't been claimed yet.

Four orcs squat fifteen feet away, gnawing scorched meat from broken bones. Stuck on a pole at the edge of a fire, the severed head of the blond-haired deserter, Alix, stares out at nothing with sightless eyes.

You groan and roll over. The hard ball of the Dragon's Eye presses into your stomach. The leather cord has snapped, causing the pouch to slip from around your neck. You're surprised the orcs haven't found it yet, but with the capture of the tower, they have plenty of booty for the time being.

Fostyr lies awake next to you, looking thin and battered but still retaining some of his good humor. "The eye," he whispers, wincing with the pain of some deep internal wound. His face is smeared with dried blood, ash, and dirt. "Do you still have it?"

You nod, looking around in fear that some of the orcs might have overheard him. "I guess we should have retreated sooner," you say. "Now what?"

Before Fostyr can answer, the orc sentries get up and approach you. Tossing their half-gnawed bones to the ground, they cut the leather thongs around your ankles. Another orc bends over Fostyr's bonds with a saw-toothed dagger.

"Gorak want to see you," one of the orcs grunts. It leans close and grins. You choke on its foul breath. The other orcs laugh, a harsh cackling sound, then drag you to a huge tent in the center of camp.

Your mouth is dry. You look around frantically, seeing no escape. Campfires blaze in every direction. There's no place to run, no way to hide the eye.

The tent is dim inside. It reeks of the rancid oil used to waterproof it, as well as charred meat and the fifteen orcs gathered inside. One of your guards prods you in the spine with the tip of its sword.

A huge orog with purple skin sits in the middle of

the drunken orcs, laughing loudly. A raven's-head amulet dangles from a chain around its neck, marking the orog as an ally of Tyrion.

"Gorak," says one of your guards.

The orog turns. The room grows silent.

"Bring close," the orog says, standing. He belches.

Gorak's lieutenants glare at you. Baring their teeth, they curse you as your captors drag you past them. You try to think of some way to destroy the eye before the orcs discover it on you. Your guard holds its spear-point at about stomach level. If you turned suddenly and shoved yourself hard into the sharp point, per-haps the talisman would break, you think wildly.

"Where is eye?" Gorak demands, voice slurred. Stepping closer, it unsheathes its sword. It jabs the tip into the hollow of your throat. The metal blazes against your cursed skin, but the orog is too drunk to see anything clearly.

"Kill me," you say, "and you'll never find out."

"Kill you later," Gorak says, staring at you blearily. "Kill friend now maybe." Gorak pulls the sword away and presses the blade to Fostyr's neck. "Where is eye?"

"It was destroyed in the battle," Fostyr says.

"Bah!" Gorak says. Yanking the blade away, the orog smacks Fostyr in the jaw with the butt end of the sword, knocking him to his knees. Fostyr doesn't cry out. He shakes the daze from his eyes.

"Let them think," Gorak tells the guards. "If they no tell by dawn, burn out eyes. One at time. If still don't tell, cut out teeth one by one till one of them talks."

Gorak spits little flecks of chewed, bloody meat on you, then lurches away. Your guards hustle you out of the tent. They lash your feet together again, throw you to the ground and kick you in the ribs—just for fun—before wandering off to their campfire.

Dawn, you think, looking up at the sky. Not much time at all.

Go to 19.

37

Battle-weary but glad to be free of the orcs for a time, you and your companions head deeper into the tunnels, searching for a way out. You still have the Dragon's Eye safely under your tunic. You must escape from these tunnels and make your way to the city of Crockport, or at least keep the talisman safe until reinforcements can arrive to drive off the orcs.

You walk alongside Renda and Relf. Renda's determination and unflagging optimism are a blessing. You wish you'd gotten to know her better before the orcs attacked. She and her brother converse easily with each other in short, clipped sentences, as if each already knows what his or her twin is going to say. Renda holds her bow ready, while Relf carries a torch. Behind you, the rest of the group follows, muttering nervously to each other.

As you trudge along, Relf tells you how he and Renda grew up as orphans on the streets of Crockport, working together, fighting for every scrap of food. Around you, the dim tunnels hum with the low conversations of your companions, which echo in the air. After a while, the joking and camaraderie begin to degenerate into quibbling and disgruntled complaints. Fatigue is taking its toll.

You stop at a wide spot in the tunnel, just beyond a heap of rubble that fell from the ceiling long ago. "We'll rest here," you say. "It should be a good place to defend ourselves if the orcs show up."

Your companions sigh with relief, drop their packs and weapons, and slump to the floor.

"It's about time," one man says dourly. He has white-blond hair, and a jagged scar pulls at his right eyelid, adding to his peevish expression. Plopping down near a pile of dry, powdery rock, he sets a coil of rope next to him. "I hope someone remembered to bring food."

Relf opens his own pack and removes some stale bread and enough dried meat for everyone to share. "Wouldn't be without it," he says. The general mood lightens as everyone begins to eat hungrily in silence. You sit on a boulder close to the pile of rubble. Renda and Relf take seats nearby.

Relf chews on his last bite of jerky and fidgets. "I hate just sitting around. I'll go scout out what's ahead," he says, rising to his feet and picking up one of the sputtering torches.

"Wait," you say. "We should stick together."

"Oh, he'll be all right," Renda says. "He can take care of himself. He saved my life more than once back at the tower."

"I'll stay within earshot," Relf says, starting down the tunnel holding the torch out in front of him.

"I hope you're right," you say to Renda, peering uneasily down the dark tunnel as the light from the torch dwindles.

After everyone has finished eating, you offer to take the first watch while the others rest. About twenty minutes into your watch, Relf returns, and you breathe easier.

"What did you find?" you ask him quietly, trying not to wake the others. Renda stirs, glances up, and smiles at her brother. Then, reassured, she goes back to sleep, her coppery hair pooled around her face.

"There's a branch in the tunnel a little way down," he says. "I can't tell which way might be most likely to lead us out, but at least I didn't spot any orcs."

"Good work," you say.

Relf sits next to you, leaning against the wall. His eyes close, but not all the way, as if he's got too much nervous energy to fall asleep.

You can't remember the last time you slept. It seems like days. The eye hangs heavy around your neck, a burden you're not sure you're stong enough to carry.

When your watch ends, you wake Renda and grate-

fully wrap yourself in your cloak. Despite your
exhaustion, sleep comes slowly. Every noise echoing
in the tunnels sounds as if it might be an oncoming
party of orcs. You fall into a fitful dream in which you
are running through dark tunnels that never end.
Monstrous footsteps thunder behind you. They grow
louder and louder until they reach a deafening roar.

Suddenly your eyes snap open.

"A cave-in!" someone shouts.

You jump to your feet. Part of the passage you
came through earlier has collapsed. Dust clogs your
lungs and makes your eyes sting.

You take a quick head count. Three of your companions are missing, one of them the blond-haired
soldier with the scar. If you can't rescue them from
the rubble quickly, the scarred soldier will never com-
plain again.

Renda and the others are already digging at the
mound of dirt and stone blocking the rear of the tunnel, and you hurry to join them. The rocks tear at
your fingers, and grit in the air stings your eyes. You
unsheathe your oaken sword and use it like a lever to
pry aside some of the heavier chunks of rock. A tiny
shower of dirt and pebbles dribbles from the tunnel
ceiling.

"This rock is unstable," you say. "We've got to
hurry before there's another cave-in."

Renda pushes aside a boulder to reveal an arm.
"Relf, help me!" she cries out. Everyone digs faster,
exposing a shoulder, then a head. The scarred man
with the white-blond hair coughs and gasps as you
burrow quickly, freeing him from the dirt. You drag
him off to one side and prop him against the tunnel
wall.

The soldier takes a huge breath, spitting dirt out of
his mouth and grumbling. "I'm all right," he says. He
motions for you to keep digging. "Save the others."

You return to the pile, but now it's become difficult
to make any progress at all. As soon as you scrape

aside some rubble, more slides down to take its place.

"It's no use," one of your companions mumbles. "They've been buried too long."

"Keep digging," Renda urges between gritted teeth. Dust coats her hair and her sweat-smudged face.

"We can't give up as long as there's hope," Relf insists.

Your muscles ache. A boulder clatters down from above, barely missing your head.

"Over here!" shouts the flail wielder from several feet away. "A foot!"

Everyone rushes to the spot and begins to toss rocks aside furiously. More dirt trickles down from the ceiling.

This victim is buried facedown. It's a woman—you recall the tall sword fighter. Miraculously her foot moves. You dig frantically until the buried woman's legs are free. Then you and Renda pull her out. Her skin has a faint bluish cast from lack of air. She coughs, but still can't speak. Renda leads her away, supporting her.

You continue to dig for your third companion, afraid of what you'll find. After half an hour, though, you and your group finally give up. The passage farther back is completely blocked, and you allow yourself the faint hope that the missing person was on the other side of the cave-in.

Another faint rumble fills the passage.

"Get back!" you shout, motioning down the tunnel. A new slide of rocky dirt cascades over the spot where you were just working.

"We're only making it worse," the scarred man says from where he sits recovering.

"There's nothing we can do now," Renda says. "I'm an optimist, but we've got to face facts. It's time to save ourselves."

And you know you must keep the eye safe at all costs. "Agreed. Let's move on."

Renda stares at the fresh pile of rubble. Relf nods reluctantly.

You and your companions set off down the tunnel, silently mourning your lost comrade. You have all lost good friends since the orc siege began. Renda helps the slowly recovering swordswoman. The scarred man hobbles along on his own, leaning into the wall occasionally for support.

Soon Relf leads you to the fork in the tunnels he found earlier. The main passage continues straight ahead, smooth and solid, large enough to walk in without stooping. A smaller tunnel angles off to the left, strewn with small heaps of crumbly white rock. The roof is so low only a child would be able to walk upright.

"So which way do we go?" the stooped flail wielder asks. "The easy way or the hard way?"

Renda creases her brow. Beside her, Relf shrugs. "I didn't go any farther than this."

The scarred blond man steps forward, rope in hand. "I think I can help," he says. "I've been down here before, back when we were exploring the tunnels searching for the lost Dragon's Eye." He squints and leans forward. He seems to be pretending to know more than he actually does.

"Yes, I remember now. I recognize this fork. The tunnel on our left leads to a larger series of tunnels that'll take us through the Cavern of a Thousand Swords. It comes out on the shore of Whyestil Lake. There are a lot of twists and turns, but I'm certain I can find the way. At least it'll lead us out of here."

"You're sure?" you ask skeptically.

The scarred man stands up, scowling at you. "Well, I'm going that way. The rest of you can either follow me or spend the rest of your lives wandering around down here," he says. He grabs the torch from Relf.

"Where does the other tunnel go?" you ask.

"Under the tower, back to the orcs," he says—too quickly, you think. "Come on. This way." He waves his torch like a banner and disappears down the smaller passage.

If you follow the scarred man into the left-hand tunnel, go to 3.

If you press on straight ahead in the main tunnel, against the man's advice, turn to 40.

38

"Let's get out of here while we can," you decide. "Maybe the creature is satisfied . . . for now."

"Then let's go before it gets its appetite back!" Grigneth cries, grabbing an oar and putting his back into his strokes purposefully.

"What about Peri?" Beatrix asks, still holding her lance ready.

Your stomach knots, but you know there's nothing you can do for the dead swordsman . . . just as there was nothing you could have done for Fostyr. "It's too late to help him," you say. "We need to save ourselves."

You turn to Grigneth and Bresnor. "Row, you two . . . with all your strength."

The boat slices forward through the water, not fast enough to escape the water beetle but enough to buy you a little time. You take up Bresnor's bow and pull an arrow from his quiver.

The water beetle is closing fast. Bright ripples of water fan out behind it. You tear a strip of cloth from your sleeve and hold your forearm out to Beatrix. "Cut me," you say.

She stares at you for a second in astonishment, then suddenly nods in comprehension. She takes out her short, sharp dagger and draws the metal blade across your skin. The cut burns with all the fury of Tyrion's curse. You bite back a scream and clamp the rag over your arm before the wound can cauterize. Blood seeps into the cloth.

"Hurry, Corlen!" Grigneth cries, staring past you, wide eyed.

The cloth hangs limp, saturated with your blood. You wrap the rag around the tip of the arrow. Nocking the arrow, you aim just ahead of the beetle.

The arrows falls short. It plunks into the water, dragging the bloody rag with it. You reach for a second arrow. Behind you, Vystan tears off a strip of his sleeve and holds it out toward you.

"No need," Beatrix says, putting one hand on your arm. "Not yet."

The water beetle slows and begins to circle the bloodied arrow. A second later, it ducks beneath the waves and disappears, following the sinking bait. You let out a breath and lower your bow.

Vystan tosses you the rag. "For the cut," he says simply.

You hold out your arm. The wound has already stopped bleeding, cauterized by Tyrion's curse. "I won't be needing it. Thanks anyway," you say.

A half hour later, there is still no sign of the water beetle. You and Beatrix take over the oars, giving Bresnor and Grigneth a much-deserved rest.

The shore of the lake slowly glides by. The uncharted forest thins, giving way to occasional huts, piers, fishing boats, and even a shore road. Before long, you are completely past the harsh wilderness, and you see the familiar outlands surrounding the city where you grew up.

You reach Crockport by nightfall, the eye still safely hidden inside your shirt. Exhausted and hungry, you and your companions tie the boat to a dock near town. The wooden buildings of the city glow with warm orange firelight, and the sounds of singing and merriment waft into the air from dockside taverns. Vystan draws a huge breath and pats his generous stomach. "Can you smell that cooking!"

Beatrix frowns. "I smell dead fish under the docks."

Gripping the lump of the package beneath your

jerkin, you step out of the boat and climb up onto a solid, well-used pier. The others follow you as you stop from time to time, looking around the lakeside buildings, getting your bearings.

Back at the tower, Captain Jongh told you to deliver the Dragon's Eye to Count Delwyn, one of the most powerful nobles in Crockport. The count's castle sits on the summit of a hill south of town, too far to go without getting some food and rest first.

"I'm starving," Vystan says.

"I think we're all in similar shape," you answer. "Let's find an inn, get something to eat, and rest for a bit. It's still a long trek up to the count's castle."

As you lead your party into the city, the familiar streets bring back a rush of memories, most of them pleasant, some of them not. Your father's sword-making smithy was just down this street. . . .

You push those memories from your mind. Each one ends with the wizard Tyrion killing your father.

Ahead of you stands the Rusty Fishhook Inn. It's old and shabby, as are most of the buildings in this part of Crockport, but the fire looks warm and the food smells good. It will have to do. You and the others are too tired and hungry to walk any farther.

Off-key singing issues from the Fishhook's open windows into the muddy street. You yank open the door and usher your companions inside. "Keep a low profile," you advise. "No need to call attention to ourselves."

The room is smoky with the pungent smell of spiced fish stew bubbling in a big kettle on the hearth.

"What have we here? Lake rats, I'll wager," says the innkeeper. "Find a table, mates. If your silver is good, my ale is better."

"And how is your food?" Vystan asks.

"Better than any you've ever tasted!" the innkeeper boasts. "You've never had anything like my fish stew."

Vystan grins and rubs his hands together in anticipation. "I love a challenge," he says. "Bring some of that stew."

Your own mouth waters. You haven't eaten anything substantial since long before you left the tower. As the innkeeper returns with a platter full of steaming bowls and mugs of ale, he leans across the bar, peering more closely at you. "Say, you look familiar," he says. "I recognize that red hair, that face. You grew up here in Crockport, didn't you?"

"I left a few years ago," you say.

"I knew it! Wasn't your father that swordmaker? The one who was killed? Let's see, your name is—"

You nod. "Corlen."

The innkeeper's voice grows soft. "Yes . . . your father used to come in here. He was a fine swordmaker and a good customer. I miss him."

"So do I," you say.

"A tragedy how he died." The bartender shakes his head, then claps his hand on your shoulder. "Enjoy the meal. The first round is on me—the ale, I mean. You'll have to pay for the stew. I can't go giving everything away, now, can I?"

Vystan slurps from the bowl and smacks his lips. "Now, this is something to sink your teeth into!"

Grigneth and Bresnor fall to their own bowls like starving animals, while Beatrix gulps down an entire tankard of ale. As you lean over to take a bite of your own stew, you notice a shabbily clad figure sitting at a nearby table watching you closely. You glance away, uneasy under the stranger's watchful gaze, and pretend not to notice as you begin to eat.

After the third round of ale, Vystan leans back in his chair and burps loudly. Beatrix laughs at him. Bresnor mutters under his breath, "Slob."

Vystan blinks at him, but his good humor gets the better of him. He chuckles and downs the remains of his tankard. He shakes his tattered sleeve at Bresnor. "Yes," he says. "Maybe so. I didn't have time to dress for dinner."

This time, even Bresnor smiles.

Still uneasy, you look around the inn, trying to enjoy the boisterous song and laughter from the other customers. Many of the faces look familiar to you. Then your gaze returns to the shabbily clad stranger.

He now stands by the back door of the Rusty Fishhook Inn. When he catches your eye, he beckons to you. He looks furtively to one side and gestures for you to follow him into the shadows, then steps out into the night.

You think for a minute. The burden of the Dragon's Eye weighs heavily on you. You're suspicious, but you're also curious. Does the stranger have something important to tell you, or is he one of Tyrion's spies, trying to lead you into a trap?

If you want to hear what the stranger has to say, turn to 32.

If you don't trust the stranger and choose to ignore him, go to 13.

39

Tyrion advances confidently. You point your oaken sword at him and back away slowly, looking for a way out of the camp. You flash a glance at Fostyr, who pales at the approach of the wizard.

There's no escape. The orcs have formed a circle around you and Fostyr, taunting you but refusing to harm you . . . because Tyrion has marked you as his own victim. Fostyr stands at your side, axe ready.

The polished wooden hilt of your sword feels slick in your hand. Heat from the orc bonfires draws beads of sweat to your forehead. You stand firm, confronting the man you hate more than anyone else in the world.

"Wood against metal," Tyrion says. "Not much of a contest."

"Wood can kill as well as steel," you reply evenly.

The orcs laugh and snort. Fostyr tightens his grip

on the axe.

Tyrion rolls his eyes at your bravado. "Yes. And your flesh will burn like wood under the fire of your father's sword." He is nearly within reach of your sword tip now.

You lunge forward suddenly, hoping to catch him off guard. Your oaken blade clacks harmlessly off the steel blade forged by your father. He was a master swordmaker, and you know your simple practice blade can never win against the rune-etched sword.

You leap back, expecting a counterattack from Tyrion. Instead, the wizard raises his free hand, and his fingers weave a spell in the air. When he is done, an afterimage of his gestures hangs in midair in front of him.

Suddenly the tip of your sword explodes in flame. The searing blaze engulfs the blade, leaving behind only charred ash, which crumbles and drifts to the ground. You're left holding the hilt. You drop it in the dirt at your feet.

The orcs whoop with delight.

"Your father's sword will turn you to ash the same way," Tyrion says calmly. "There'll be nothing left of you but dust."

You fumble for your whip. Perhaps you can blind Tyrion with a swift stroke.

Tyrion smiles. "Why not fight with a real sword, Corlen?" He turns to the orcs. "Would one of you gentlemen be kind enough to lend Corlen your sword so he has a proper weapon to fight with?"

You look around. The orcs raise a forest of metal blades. Steel, iron . . . all cursed. The orcs clatter them against their shields. You can almost feel the metal burning your skin. You can touch none of the offered weapons, and Tyrion knows it. Breathing heavily, you glare at Tyrion.

"What's the matter, Corlen?" the wizard asks, his mouth twisted in cruel amusement. He takes another step closer. "Afraid to do what is necessary to kill me?" He waits a second, then snorts in disgust. "Grab him," he orders several nearby orcs.

Fostyr moves to intercept them, but you put a hand on his arm. "Don't give them the satisfaction," you say. "They'll kill you where you stand."

Two orcs grab your arms from behind, holding them tightly in their gnarled hands. A second pair of orcs grasp Fostyr's arms, wrenching Gorak's axe from his hands and tossing it to the ground.

Tyrion steps close to you. His hot breath tickles your face. "Let's conduct a little test," he says, "to see how well my curse has held up over the years."

He raises the tip of the blade in front of your eyes, flicking the tip from side to side. You tense, anticipating the agonizing touch.

Tyrion holds the blade even closer to your face. He touches your eyelashes, then drops the tip an inch lower to brush your cheek. Just a touch. You hiss and wince as a lightning flash of pain jolts you. You swallow the scream rising in your throat as the smell of your own burned flesh rises to your nostrils.

"The curse seems as good as new," Tyrion says. "But I'd better be sure." He touches the tip to your other cheek, and again you flinch, as if scorched by a red-hot iron.

You shake your head. "You're a coward, Tyrion," you say through clenched teeth. "Everyone here can see it. I can't believe the orcs accept you as their leader."

The orcs around you grumble. "Let him fight," one calls out.

Tyrion glances at the disgruntled orcs, then whirls and plunges the sword into the ground. The long sword quivers in the dirt, standing upright. The wizard steps away from it, arms spread wide.

"Fair enough," Tyrion says. He gestures for the two orcs to release you. They relax their grip.

"Fight good," one of them grumbles.

You step up to the beautifully crafted blade and

SIEGE OF THE TOWER

stop, staring down at it. With one stroke you could take off Tyrion's head, but the sword might as well as be a hundred miles away. You can't touch it. Fostyr watches you helplessly.

"Go on," Tyrion taunts. "Take the sword. Draw it out and strike me down. Or are *you* the coward?"

You stand frozen, knowing that if you wield the sword, it will sear your hands to the bone. The pain from even the brief kiss of metal still throbs in your cheeks.

You shake your head, and the nearest orcs spit at you and howl derisively. "You know I can't," you say to Tyrion. You ignore the orcs. The wizard is your real enemy.

"No?" Tyrion says. "Maybe you need a little more incentive."

He yanks the sword from the ground and walks to where the two orcs hold Fostyr motionless only a few feet away from you.

You stiffen. Your fingers brush the whip handle hanging from your belt. If you move fast enough, you might be able to keep Tyrion from killing your friend. And maybe, if you're lucky, you can wrap the whip around Tyrion's neck.

Or maybe you should go for the sword. Perhaps you could endure the pain and the crippling burns long enough to strike down Tyrion. After that, what else matters?

Tyrion holds the blade's edge against Fostyr's throat. The honed surface presses into the young man's skin just above his jugular vein.

If you leap forward and grab Tyrion's sword, turn to 42.

If you grab for your whip, go to 26.

40

Leaving the scarred man behind, you push him out of your thoughts as you continue ahead down the passage. The others follow you in uneasy silence.

Your meager supplies of food are gone. You come across tiny, lime-encrusted puddles, but the water is undrinkable. You are thirsty, your lips dry and cracked from all the digging through the dusty rubble after the cave-in. If you don't find a way out of the caverns soon, the Dragon's Eye talisman will be lost with you, buried again in the labyrinth where it had remained hidden for so many centuries. You smile grimly at the irony and wonder if that fate would be so terrible after all. At least, the eye wouldn't fall into Tyrion's hands. But that would be small consolation if you and all your companions had to perish to accomplish it.

After several hours, you realize that you're hopelessly lost, but you dare not show it. You've passed so many caves and new tunnels that you can't remember if you've seen them before or not. They all look the same. You wonder what time it is. Days could pass and you'd never know.

The torches are starting to burn feebly. Without the torches, you're doomed. You order a few of them to be snuffed out, hoping to make them last longer. Relf, in the lead, continues to carry one of the few torches left burning.

When you come to the next branching of tunnels, you call a halt. Everyone is exhausted; no one is thinking straight. You need your companions to be alert. You send Renda and Turloc to scout the tunnel in one direction.

"Report back in five minutes," you instruct them.

Renda nods wearily and heads off. You and Relf check the second tunnel.

Five minutes later, you and Relf rejoin Renda and the flail wielder. Renda reports that their tunnel is partially caved in.

"It just doesn't look safe," she says, shifting the bow on her shoulder. "I think we should take the other tunnel."

"Fine," you say. The tunnel you and Relf followed opens into a warm, dry chamber, large enough to hold everyone comfortably. You set up camp there.

To conserve torches, you put out all but the one the person who stands watch will use. Assigning Relf the first watch, you curl up on the rocky cave floor. You roll part of your cloak under your head for a pillow, then pull a fold of it over your shoulders as a blanket, but the cave is still dank and cold. Luckily you're so tired that your discomfort doesn't matter. You drift off to sleep, thinking that hard stone never felt so comfortable.

A faint singsong murmur, mingling with the snores of your companions, wakes you. There's no light, not even from the wavering torch. Relf has let it burn out!

You move your fingers in front of your eyes, but you can't see them. You touch your face but still can't see your hands. The darkness around you is absolutely complete and impenetrable. A chill spreads through you, raising goose bumps on your neck and arms.

"Relf?" you whisper. "Relf, you're supposed to be on watch!" Hearing no answer, you call louder. "Relf!"

Nothing. A few of the others stir restlessly but continue to sleep.

You wrap the cloak around you, feeling your way to the wall. You hear the faint murmur again. It sounds like voices. Brushing your fingertips along the wall, you carefully place one foot in front of the other as you head down the corridor in the direction of the voices. "Relf?" you say again.

Several minutes later, you turn a corner in the passageway. You see weak light flickering ahead. You creep toward it, like a moth drawn to a flame. Soon an arched doorway appears in the side of the tunnel. The voices seem to be coming from there.

"Power," they sing. "Riches. Land."

You approach cautiously. The words draw you closer. Relf stands just inside the doorway as if hypnotized, the torch hanging limply in his right hand. His bronze hair shimmers, and his eyes glint as he stares in awe.

"There you are, Relf!" you cry. Relieved, you step through the doorway into a cavern dotted with glittering jewels: rubies, diamonds, emeralds, amethysts. Sapphire crystals larger than your arm, gleaming opals like crystallized milk, tiger's-eyes, garnets . . . every kind of gem you have ever imagined.

His mouth hanging open, Relf stares at his left hand. It's filled with a rainbow of gems. The singing changes, filling your ears.

> *"Hear the truth,*
> *or your heart's desire.*
> *Clearly see,*
> *or dream and expire."*

"Relf," you say, more insistently this time. You shake him, but he doesn't respond. He seems to be under some kind of spell. Which did the young archer choose, you wonder—truth or desire? If you make the same choice, you'll end up the same way, transfixed and mindless.

You turn to get help but find you can't move. Your legs seem to be fastened to the floor. You can't get away. You must choose.

After a pause you say out loud to the mysterious voices, "I want to hear the truth. I want to see clearly."

Maybe that will tell you how to free Relf.

Within seconds, the gems vanish and the singing turns to shrieks of fury. Instead of a vast cavern, you find yourself standing in a tiny, cramped room chiseled out of rough stone.

Relf holds a few dirty pebbles in his hand. Skeletons of dwarves, orcs, and humans litter the floor. Obviously they made the wrong choice and saw only what they wanted to see, not what was really there.

You can move your legs once more. Quickly you dump the pebbles from Relf's hand and start to drag him toward the door. He doesn't struggle. He simply remains limp, as if stunned.

The voices in the air shriek louder, buffeting you like a shrill wind. Cries of misery chill you to the bone. Shivering, you stagger out into the passage.

As soon as you pass through the arch, the voices fade to a whisper. Relf shudders, looking up at you in confusion.

The voices vanish.

"I heard . . . someone," he says, puzzled. "What happened?"

You explain the curse as you return to your companions. Relf hangs his head, embarrassed.

"I wanted to see all the things I'll never have," he says apologetically. "Renda should have been there with me."

"It's all right," you say, placing a hand on his shoulder. "It's over now. It doesn't matter."

You wake Renda and ask her to stand the next watch. You warn her about the voices. Then you settle down next to Relf. He's still awake.

"Go to sleep," you say.

"I'm afraid to," he says. "What if I dream and never wake up?"

"Dreams can't hurt you," you tell him. "It's only bad if you see nothing *but* dreams. You have to face reality."

He nods and closes his eyes, but his breathing is ragged for a long time. Finally it evens out into restful sleep. At last you can get some rest yourself.

You and the others wake refreshed. You light an extra torch and set out again. Your head seems clearer now. The side passages and branchings in the main tunnel don't all look the same anymore. You wind your way through the labyrinth, choosing the passages that slope up—to the surface, you hope.

After an hour, you come to a level intersection. You seem to be faced with two equal choices. The inside of one tunnel is shiny and sticky to the touch, barely large enough to crawl through. An unpleasant odor, one you can't place, fills the tunnel.

The walls of the other passage feel warm—almost hot. Small puddles of acrid-smelling liquid dot the floor. The odor makes your eyes water.

Squatting next to one of the puddles, you pull a thread from your cloak and lower it into the fluid. The thread immediately sizzles and dissolves.

Acid. Powerful acid.

Relf stands by your side, holding the torch ahead of him at arm's length. Together you peer down the passage. The acid puddles are spaced far enough apart that you can avoid them if you're careful.

"Not much of a choice," Renda says.

You glance at the torches. They're almost burned out. You don't have much time to escape the caves.

"We can't go back," you say.

Renda and Relf nod in agreement. But which tunnel should you choose?

If you elect to go down the shiny, sticky tunnel, turn to 15.
If you decide to follow the smooth tunnel dotted with acid puddles, turn to 17.

41

You find yourself in a firelit courtyard with rock walls on three sides. The count's castle forms the fourth, rising tall and formidable, with perfectly matched stone blocks. The archers on the parapet turn from the wall, tracking you with their half-drawn bows.

"Why are they so suspicious of us?" Grigneth whispers in a whining voice.

"Maybe they can smell you're a coward," Beatrix answers, leaning closer to him.

Another tense minute passes in which no one speaks. You look up past the thick barricade walls at the sky and notice streaks of light in the east from the approaching dawn. "I hope they give us something to eat," Vystan says. "I didn't get to finish my supper."

Without a sound, a tall man walks out of a shadowed gate at the edge of the courtyard far to your right. He steps into the brighter light of the courtyard, clad in the azure cloak of a count in the Kingdom of Furyondy. You recognize him at once, though his hair is now silver-gray. When you were younger, it was jet black. You realize how long it has been since you've been back to Crockport.

Count Delwyn approaches you and smiles. "If Corrh the swordmaker was your father, you are always welcome at my castle. Many of my fighters still use weapons forged by your father's hand. Good, strong weapons." He looks you over carefully.

"You look much like your father . . . the same red hair, the same gray eyes."

Your throat aches at the memory of your father and makes it impossible to speak for the moment.

Count Delwyn nods at the pouch you hold in your hand. "I understand you have something for me. Captain Jongh sent you from Dragon's Eye Tower?"

You clear your throat. "Yes, sir," you say. "The tower is beseiged by an orc army, and it may already have fallen. The reinforcements didn't arrive in time, and so my companions and I were charged to take the Dragon's Eye to safety and to deliver it into your protection."

You work at the laces around the pouch, tugging it open. You step forward to hand it to him, relieved that you can finally deliver the Dragon's Eye and be rid of the burden, knowing the magic artifact will not fall into the hands of the forces of Iuz.

"Wait!" someone shouts from off to your left. It sounds as if Count Delwyn has spoken, but the count stands directly in front of you.

You turn . . . and see another Count Delwyn step from the shadows. An exact duplicate. You freeze and then, thinking fast, you snatch the pouch back from the first count's grasp.

"You'll never get the eye, Tyrion," the second count says. "No matter what trickery you use."

You take a step back. Beatrix holds her lance at the ready. Vystan pulls out his flail and whirls it around his head. Bresnor readies his longbow, while Grigneth hangs back, looking confused.

"Don't believe him!" the first count says, glaring at the duplicate. His face contorts in anger. "He's the evil sorcerer Tyrion in disguise. He's trying to trick you into giving him the eye."

His gaze returns to you. "If you let him have the eye, Corlen, you'll bring tragedy to all the land."

The second count smiles, shaking his head. "You're the one who will bring tragedy upon us, imposter. Did you think I would lie sick forever while you took my place and gave false orders in my name?"

Bewildered, the count's guards grumble on the parapets, pointing their arrows from one target to the other. Your companions stand ready to fight. The captain of the guard stares in disbelief. "Even I can't tell the difference," he says. "Do you mean I might have been serving the wrong man?"

"I can understand your confusion," the second count says, raising his voice so that all his guards can hear. "Maybe this will help convince you that I can be trusted." He motions with his hand, and Fostyr steps out of the shadows behind him.

Your jaw drops. Your companions cry out in surprise. Tears sting your eyes as you hurry toward your old friend. Clapping his back, you shake your head in confusion. "Fostyr! How did you survive the battle with the orcs? How did you escape?"

"How did you get here?" Beatrix asks from behind you.

But something is wrong. Fostyr doesn't react. He doesn't even seem to recognize you. Instead, he simply stands stiffly beside the second count, staring straight ahead with glassy eyes. You draw back, confused. The blank look in his eyes frightens you.

"He's my friend, but he doesn't seem to know me," you say, turning to the second count. "What's wrong with him? How on earth did he get here?"

"My hunters found him wandering in Vesve Forest yesterday. He was entranced, just as you see him now," the second count says. "They brought him to me, and I recognized him at once. I seem to recall, Corlen, that his family lived near yours?"

You nod uncertainly, but the first count curses. "Liar! The boy can't speak because you put a spell on him. Now you're using him to entice this young fighter into giving you the eye. Why don't you release him from your spell, wizard, and see what Fostyr himself has to say about you?"

"Speak for yourself," says the second count. "You're the one who has used ensorcellment for your own evil purposes. Otherwise you wouldn't be able to look so much like me."

The count's guards continue to point their weapons from one target to the other, still baffled.

"Enough of this!" you shout. You study each count carefully, trying to decide which is the real Count Delwyn and which is Tyrion. Count Delwyn's hunters *could* have found Fostyr in the forest, but in his present condition, how could your friend ever have escaped? On the other hand, Tyrion could have taken Fostyr from his orc captors, intending to use him as a decoy here, a last chance to get the eye.

You bite your lip. If only you could break the spell on your friend, even for a moment. He would tell you which is the real count.

You step back, still searching Fostyr's eyes for some clue, but you see nothing. His eyes are empty and frighteningly lifeless.

Your oaken sword shifts against your thigh. As you grip the hilt, a solution comes to you. You glance at the two counts. Both wear swords under their blue cloaks, but Tyrion will be wearing the sword forged by your father, the sword with magical runes carved into the blade, which enable the wizard to wield the sword with a trained fighter's skill. Rumor has it that the spell-enhanced sword can cut through anything, including stone and metal. It could even kill a wizard.

Tyrion might be able to disguise the appearance of the sword, but not its power.

"I won't give up the eye until I'm sure who the true Count Delwyn is," you say. You look around the courtyard until you spot a large iron anvil, gouged and nicked from years of hammering, but still solid.

"Bring that anvil over here," you tell Vystan and Beatrix.

"What are you doing?" asks the first count.

Straining under the anvil's weight, Beatrix and Vystan set it on the flagstones in front of you.

"You will each hand over your sword to Beatrix. She will try to cleave this anvil. That will tell us who the real count is."

"A sword can't cleave an anvil," protests the second count.

"One sword can," you say.

You nod to Beatrix. She steps up to the first count, holding her hand out to accept his sword.

"This is an outrage!" the first count complains. His hand clasps the hilt of his sword. "No Count of Furyondy has ever given up his sword while there is still breath in his body! Don't come any closer."

"Tyrion," you mutter under your breath. Beatrix pauses, glancing back at you. You turn toward the second Delwyn, ready to hand him the eye, but then you hesitate. You might as well put him to the test, too.

"Beatrix," you say, nodding toward the second count. "One sword will tell us as much as two."

As Beatrix approaches, the second count slides his sword out of his scabbard. "Not you," he says to Beatrix. "No Count of Furyondy has given his weapon to a stranger. I agree to relinquish my sword for this test, but only to one I trust, one who would never use it against me." He turns and fixes you with his gaze. "I will give it to you, Corlen, and only to you."

Clever, you think. Tyrion knows you can't take his metal sword without burning your hands. But the real count might not know about the curse and innocently offer the sword to you.

The guards are getting restless. You need to make your decision soon. Which count should you trust? You glance from one to the other, attempting to see into each man's heart.

If you choose to give the eye to the first count, turn to 24.

If you decide to give the eye to the second count, go to 11.

42

You launch yourself at Tyrion, concentrating on the sword he holds in his hand. "Stop!" you shout.

Your only thought is to save Fostyr. You force every other thought aside, not allowing yourself to imagine the agony you'll experience the moment your fingers touch the metal hilt. Fostyr sacrificed himself so you could escape. He did it knowing he would probably die. Now it's your turn to do the same for him.

With a burst of speed, you wrap your hands around the hilt of the sword, and for a second your anger blots out the expected pain.

In that same frozen moment, Tyrion gapes at you, stunned, as if he can't believe you're foolish enough to attack him. He barely has time to blink in shock and astonishment before the two of you tumble to the ground, the sword gripped in both of your hands.

You land on top of the wizard. Your weight knocks the breath out of Tyrion. You wrestle the blade from his hands.

For the first time since your father died, you hold a real metal sword in your hands. It's lighter than you remember it, but well balanced. The blade feels like a natural extension of your arms, as if it has always been a part of you. The metal seems to sing in your hands.

Jaw clenched, you wait for the blistering jolt of pain that will fuse your hands to the hilt.

Instead, a flash of light fills the air, and you hear a loud thunderclap. Tyrion shrieks, rolling out from under you. He claws at the dirt, scrabbling to get away like a startled lizard.

Your hands tingle with contained energy, but you experience no pain. Your fingers feel strong, full of power. Everything seems to stop for a second as you stare at your hands in disbelief.

Anger couldn't have removed the curse. Maybe it was your fear for Fostyr, or your willingness to give your life to save his. . . .

The orcs surge into motion, as if suddenly snapped out of their stupor. Half of them flee, shrieking, vanishing into the forest beyond the firelight.

You push yourself to one knee, glaring at the remaining orcs. Hatred and fear etch their faces. They clench and unclench their weapons, uncertain what to do. They are terrified of you.

Tyrion rises, his hands trembling at his sides. His face is a mask of rage.

"My sword!" he says, his lips quivering. "Your father forged it for me, and I made it what it is now."

He hurls himself at you. His cloak flutters behind him, and his arms spread wide like the grotesque wings of some ravenous vulture.

You raise the throbbing sword. Unable to stop his headlong plunge, the wizard impales himself on the shimmering blade. The force of Tyrion's momentum knocks you backward onto the ground.

He crashes on top of you, light as a skeleton. Blackish blood froths from his mouth. The carrion stench of his breath convulses your stomach. His fingers claw maniacally at your eyes, still trying to kill you even though his wound is surely mortal. His eyes, rimmed with red, blaze in their sockets. You wince. You feel as if you're staring into the eyes of a fiend.

Then the blaze fades. Now you stare into the watery eyes of a dying old man.

Tyrion coughs. The sound vibrates through the blade of the sword and into your hands. The wizard's life sputters and fades away.

You shove Tyrion's lifeless body off of you like so much firewood, then yank the blade from his chest. The corpse shrivels, then collapses into itself until there's nothing left but a pile of bones, hidden by the wizard's night-black cloak. A mask of dried skin stretches over his skull.

Head down, you kneel on one knee beside the body. "At last you're avenged, Father," you whisper.

You look up when you hear the rattle of weapons. Snarling and bellowing, the remaining orcs have recovered their courage and surge forward, intent on killing you.

You rise quickly. Fostyr retrieves Gorak's axe and rushes to your side. Your father's sword feels impossibly light in your hands. You imagine you can wield it for hours before tiring.

Somehow, by selflessly risking pain for the sake of another person, by putting Fostyr's life above your own, you have broken Tyrion's curse. But you have no time to revel in the new feeling right now. Guarding each other's back, you and Fostyr meet the oncoming orcs.

A huge orc raises an iron mace, swinging it at your head. Your enhanced blade slices through the iron haft and continues into the orc's chest.

Another creature lunges at you with a spiked club. You block the club with your sword. The blade vibrates from the impact, but you slash sideways across the orc's face, blinding the creature.

The metal tip of a spear grazes your left arm from behind. Pain shoots through your arm, but it isn't the red-hot pain of magical fire from the curse. You parry a second thrust, shattering the spear's shaft, then run the orc through.

You taste grit between your teeth, and hot sweat stings your eyes. Smoke from the bonfire next to you billows into the air.

Suddenly a battle horn sounds from the black depths of the forest. A volley of arrows hails down among the orcs. Their steel tips flash like raindrops in the light of the campfires.

Battle cries mix with orc screams of pain. The orcs glance wildly around for the new enemy. One creature breaks for the woods. Another follows.

Seconds later, with no leader to hold them together, all the orcs are in full retreat. They trip over the bodies of their fallen comrades. A few never get up, victims of the next volley of arrows.

In minutes, they have completely abandoned their camp, leaving behind a shambles of collapsed tents, scattered fires, and discarded weapons. You and Fostyr turn to face each other. Fostyr drops his axe and grins. You grin back.

Shouts echo from around the camp. You tense, then relax as familiar faces step into the firelight. The rest of your party has returned. You knew they wouldn't let you down.

You laugh out loud with the release of tension. Your comrades gather round you, clapping you on the back and examining your father's sword in awe.

You close your eyes. The Dragon's Eye tugs at your neck. For a moment, you had forgotten about it. It seems as heavy as always, but soon you will deliver it to Count Delwyn.

It's too good to be true. Fostyr is alive, the curse that has haunted you for most of your life is broken, and Tyrion is dead. Your father is avenged, and his sword has been returned to you.

It's as if you've stepped through fire and come out reforged.

Still grinning, Fostyr rubs his hands together. "Well, what do we do now?" he asks, pretending to be bored.

"How about taking on Iuz himself?" you joke with a broad grin.

The End